LEX

James Mylet is 34 years old. You don't need to know more than that.

James Mylet

LEX

Quercus

First published in Great Britain in 2011 by

Quercus
21 Bloomsbury Square
London
WC1A 2NS

Copyright © 2011 by James Mylet

The moral right of James Mylet to be identified as the author of this work has been asserted in accordance with the Copyright, Designs and Patents Act, 1988.

All rights reserved. No part of this publication may be reproduced or transmitted in any form or by any means, electronic or mechanical, including photocopy, recording, or any information storage and retrieval system, without permission in writing from the publisher.

A CIP catalogue record for this book is available from the British Library

ISBN (TPBO) 978 0 85738 067 8

This book is a work of fiction. Names, characters, businesses, organizations, places and events are either the product of the author's imagination or are used fictitiously. Any resemblance to actual persons, living or dead, events or locales is entirely coincidental.

1 0 9 8 7 6 5 4 3 2 1

Typeset by Ellipsis Books Limited, Glasgow
Printed and bound in Great Britain by Clays Ltd, St Ives plc

For Catherine & Felix

1

TUESDAY 2ND MAY 2006

It takes me eight minutes to get from school back to my house. The bell goes at 12.10 p.m., and as I'm sixth year I get to go out of grounds at lunch. If I'm not held up I get home for 12.20 p.m. I'll grab a banana, some orange juice, butter some bread, stuff some ham on it and I can be at the computer in my room for the 12.30 p.m. broadcast.

The computer will have played through the track list I set running when I left in the morning. I'll fade out the last song nearest to 12.30 p.m. and say something like, 'Afternoon everybody, howareya? I'm Lex Donal and welcome to the lunchtime show on Radio Clifden. In about fifteen minutes we'll be havin' a shufti at the headlines, then I'll read out a few of your messages, let you know what's going on this evening and a few of the songs you can be looking forward to this afternoon before I'm back to school.'

I'll fade up the next track and take a moment to eat my

lunch, whilst I look through the texts and email messages that have come in during the morning.

Mrs O'Dowd, who works at Matherson's, a shop that sells clothes and strange tat to meandering tourists and occasional locals, has asked for a Take That song this afternoon. She asks for a Take That song every afternoon. In the mid Nineties I reckon they awakened a sexual desire in the post-menopausal woman that I fear she wishes to cherish. I will drop it in the playlist this afternoon but I don't always do it; I can't be seen to be pandering to the audience, but she is a friend of me Ma's though, so if I don't do it regularly enough she'll mention it to Ma and I'll get to hear about it.

I'm thinking of making a jingle just for her, announcing it as 'Mrs O'Dowd's Take That time'. I could get her to come in and record a few introductions for the songs. I should write that idea down.

The next song comes to an end; it's Prince's 'Cream'. I fade it down and press pause on the playlist, before looking out of the window to announce that this May 2nd is looking to be a soft day, thank god. The clouds are a light downy grey and there'll probably be rain later as there usually is, but remember that's what keeps this beautiful county of Connemara looking so lush and green.

The next song is by Bon Jovi. Bon Jovi can suck my balls for all I care. The music I play isn't totally to my taste but I have to always keep my audience in mind, and the audience who listens to Radio Clifden is very diverse, from teenagers in their bedrooms to shop workers in their sixties to office workers in their forties, so there has got to be something for everyone, and there has to be something for me too, obviously.

Naturally I make sure I abuse my position as the only radio station for miles around by making them listen to songs I like. What's the point of having a radio station if you can't inflict your musical preferences on others, and with enough exposure the listeners actually come round to and possibly even *like* acts they would never have heard of. I like the idea of the workers at the freight warehouse shuffling along badly to some ska on a Tuesday afternoon in a remote town in the west of Ireland, 3,000 miles and forty years from where and when it was first recorded.

I have to remember not to play anything too extreme though, as that's the stuff that makes people switch off. The bland stuff flows right over them, they don't even notice it. It's the opposite with me; the bland stuff makes me want to smash the radio in.

I scan the RTE website for the news headlines, which I read out as close to quarter to the hour as possible. I check the playlist for the afternoon and that there are enough songs dragged and dropped to cover it all. I paste in a couple of ads too.

Before I sign off and get back to school I set the afternoon puzzler. This afternoon it is: 'How many colours are there in a rainbow? And we should know that, as we get more rainbows than anywhere else in the world right here in Connemara, yes we do and that is a Lex Fact.'

A 'Lex Fact' they know is anything I make up and can't prove.

'I'll be back at half four, in time for the home stretch, be seeing you all then,' and I switch back to the playlist.

So that's my lunchtime. I go down the stairs in two jumps, using the banister and wall to help me swing down, pick up my bag and then head off back to school. Economics class this afternoon. I did my homework this time so it should be no bother.

As school subjects go I like Economics the best; it's sort of about people and predicting what they do. Besides if I'm going to live in London, I'll have to know about business: everyone knows about it in the City. I should start getting the London *FT*, I think. I'll talk to me Da about getting it when he gets home tonight.

Yeah, so that's me and me radio station. I mean it's a pirate radio station, it's not like it's proper proper; it's just me in my bedroom playing some songs from my computer. I started it two years ago just playing music on a small signal so people in our town would have something on FM to listen to. That's the problem with us in Clifden: we're miles from anywhere, on the real arse end of the west coast. The FM signals from Galway don't usually carry all the way out to us, so we get the occasional medium wave radio stations but they don't really play much music.

So that's when I decided to start Radio Clifden. I have a huge collection of music that I ripped off the Internet and downloaded from BitTorrent and sites like Kazaa or LimeWire. I've got like 5,000 songs stored on my computer so I've got plenty of tracks.

I started off just playing songs then moved on to recording the odd jingle, just the odd 'You're listening to Radio Clifden, where the music is just for you,' cheesy, no? But I just wanted something so that they knew it was coming from their area, that they could identify with.

My little brother Sean does a freebie paper round, so I printed up some flyers and used him to drop them off with his papers with the setting 106.5 FM on them, and I dropped one through the letter boxes of all the shops in town one evening.

The broadcasts were only when I came home from school from 4 to 6 p.m. I was too nervous to actually say anything, and I was worried it would come out wrong, so I just concentrated on playing songs.

In the jingles I gave out the station's frequency and Hotmail address for comments. The day I got my first email was brilliant, proper exciting: it was proof people were listening. I'd been broadcasting for three weeks and I didn't know if anyone was receiving it or tuning in. I hadn't told anyone at school and no one had mentioned it to me. The email was from Martha Fenwick, she's Tommy Fenwick's mum who was in my year at school but has moved to Dublin to work as an apprentice printer. Her email just said, 'Hello,' nothing more than that, it was sweet though. 'Hello yourself, listener number one.'

Knowing people were listening started to make me worry more. I wondered how many people were listening and did they know who I was. I liked it being anonymous, no shame that way.

And of course technically it was illegal. So I did think there was a chance someone might report me if they found out who I was. But my Da is great mates with Peter O'Reilly, who is in the Garda in Clifden, and he checked it would be OK with him. Peter said as long as it doesn't interfere with any of the emergency frequencies it was fine by him. In fact he added one other proviso – 'Don't play any bloody Van Morrison.' He hated Van Morrison, something to do with the Sixties, but according to my Da if I played Van Morrison he'd set the police dog on me.

So gradually I started speaking into the microphone; back then for a microphone I used one ear of a pair of headphones that was plugged into the microphone socket. I would practise like twenty times during the song before actually saying anything.

Really simple stuff: 'Hi howareya? This is Radio Clifden, that was Red Hot Chili Peppers, and next up some Carpenters.' It was amazing how nervous I was, chronic; I now knew people were actually listening and it froze me up, not really a help if I want to be a radio DJ one day.

I wouldn't say my name for ages, so I would get people email and ask who I was. I hadn't even told the lads, as they'd destroy me if they found out, especially the stuff I was playing, they'd hate it. But then I wasn't just playing music for them; I'm playing for everyone in the town. We're a nice town in Clifden. We deserve a decent radio station: it's not our fault we're miles from anywhere.

The thing I like doing so much is getting them listening to something they wouldn't normally hear and then liking it. Like Toots and the Maytals, I love Toots and the Maytals, they're lethal, and gradually I've managed to get people in Clifden to love them too. I mean there's nothing not to love, they're deadly. I make sure once a day I stick one of their tunes on, and on Friday afternoon the last song of the week is always their version of 'Country Roads (Take Me Home)'. I put it on for all the people at work who are getting to the end of the week. It's the finishing line for them; once they hear that they can go home. Like yer man Freddie Flintstone when he hears that hooter go, time to slide down the back of a dinosaur and head on home.

It's taken off at the Harp too, Michael now puts it on at last orders. You've got until the song finishes to get your drinks order in and by then people are usually pretty drunk so they'll sing it too which is cool, kind of like 'I did that,' I made people like that.

So the day usually goes something like this: I load up the songs before school and then we go live at 8.30 a.m. I need nine and a half hours of music, that's 570 minutes, which is the golden marker to get to. I sprinkle in a few singles that I've recorded, ones like: 'You're listening to Radio Clifden on 106.5 FM,' or 'Radio Clifden – if it's not raining now, just give it another five minutes.' I had one I thought was really funny which was: 'Radio Clifden – don't tell the Gardi' but my Da thought it was cheeky so he made me take it off.

I also got a few adverts: one for O'Dea's the butcher, one for the Harp pub. Fagan's Cars have one and so do Keavey

Motors. I only put one of their ads on each per day; I don't want to bore people.

They don't pay me much: €20 here and there. I don't chase them down for the money, so they can either send it in or not. Michael at the Harp will give me a free pint if he's serving, and O'Dea's tend not to charge my mum if she goes in for a joint of meat.

So I set the music running at 8.30 a.m. before I go into school, then I come back for lunch and do the lunchtime broadcast. Finally I get back at about 3.50 p.m. and do from 4 to 6 p.m.

I sometimes do that broadcast with Davey Mahon. He's my best bud and we often record sketches after 6 p.m. for the following day, like spoof news stories or a fake history of Clifden.

We did a series about famous people who were born in Clifden and what it was like for them, growing up in the town, but it was people who were blatantly not from here. Winston Churchill, Nelson Mandela, Michael Jackson. We'd go through what they'd been like at school and interview imaginary friends they'd had growing up before they left for the big time, telling stories about how they knew Michael Jackson was destined to make it when they saw how good he was at playing hurling, a first-rate centre half-forward he was by all accounts. Fuck it, I thought it was funny.

Davey used to do a joke-a-day thing but it just didn't really work so we stopped it. I'm going to miss Davey when I go off to college. Davey's mental; his whole family is tapped and he's the product of his environment and the genes, nature and nurture both dealing him a shite hand, and so he was always on a hiding to nothing when he landed on this planet, but he's a funny lad and I like him, even if most others don't. We haven't talked too much about what he's going to do when I leave. I don't want to sound like a girl, but it's too sensitive for us to mention it and we're lads an' all, we're not like going to get all deep and emotional and all that bollocks. I hope he leaves Clifden; he talked about Dublin but I don't know what he wants to do. He works as a chef at the Continental Hotel usually from seven in the morning until three in the afternoon. He likes the craic in the kitchen and that but I want him to get out of this town if he can.

He reckons he's scuttled a waitress at the hotel. Won't tell me her name though, so I know he's lying just to cover his ass, but I guess I'm just too decent to call him on it.

That's the one thing that's bothering me before I go to London: I'm seventeen and I still haven't had a ride yet. I could of done it already definitely – there's Trisha Murphy who was in our year at school before she dropped out; she said she'd do me when she was drunk once. But she's a big unit and I don't want to do her; besides I know at least five guys who've had a go on her, so I'm not starting there.

I can't go to London a virgin; they'll all be able to tell, it'll be so embarrassing. I have a plan; so far it has done nothing for me, but what the fuck. The plan is Michelle O'Reilly; she's not related to the sergeant, and she's a total dream. She was in the year above me at school, and I've always liked her. I speak to her when I go to Super-Value; she works behind the sandwich counter. I always make sure it's her that serves me. Oh man she's lovely, you should see her; her hair is curly, tight curly, and goes down to her shoulders. It's dark brown, but her eyes are a bluey-green colour, really pale. Oh yeah and when she smiles, oh my god I mean she's gorgeous. I tell her every time I go in that I'm going to play a song for her, I know they have the radio on at the sandwich counter and they listen to us.

I can't dedicate a song in name to her though, cos she's got a boyfriend called Liam, Liam Dansey. Dansey the Pansie as no one called him at school, cos he was three years above me and absolute bullets. And he's a dick. Obviously he would have to be a dick. I'm sure I would've thought he was a dick even if he wasn't, but it just so happens that he is a dick, proper.

Maybe I could dedicate a track to her as in, 'This is for you if your boyfriend is a dick.' She's what I'm holding out for. Davey thinks I'm wasting my time and going to die a virgin. I don't want to die a virgin but there's no chance I'm going to ride some fat scraggy bike just for the sake of it. I've got standards; they're not high but I have some.

So I've got this massive few months coming up and my head's all over the shop. I've got my Leaving Certificate exams starting in two and a bit weeks' time, and if I do as well as I did in my mocks, then I'm going to the London

School of Economics to study Economics and Politics. It's also my eighteenth birthday at the end of July, and the huge news is at the end of August I'm putting on a festival for the radio station and only Toots and the bloody Maytals are coming over . . . to play . . . for us . . . in Clifden. It's going to be deadly. Seriously, Toots and the Maytals are coming to Clifden, can you believe that? I've booked the acts, booked the stage, the tent, the sound; we've got three bands as well as them, it is going to be unreal. Clifden has never had anything like it before, and if I balls it up it probably never will again.

So I kind of want it to be a goodbye and a thank you for the radio station and everything. No one wants to take on the station when I'm gone, so I think I'm just going to shut it down and stop it for good.

I've written to some proper London radio stations and have got two weeks of work experience with XFM before university starts in mid September. I tried the BBC but that was a nightmare as everyone wants in there and I heard nothing from them.

I'm bricking it at the moment; if the festival all goes tits up I'm going to leave town and never come back. I've done the tickets on my computer and have cut them out myself. I need to sell the full sixteen hundred to cover my costs. I've left them at various places over town to sell with Tupperware boxes for them to keep the money in. Matherson's has got fifty, the Harp's got fifty. I'll see how they get on. I've got to do posters soon that I'm going to put up around town and I'm going to start really plugging it on the radio station. I want them to sell out early before the tourists arrive for the summer. Actually, scratch that. I don't care who comes, I just want them to sell out. I need them to sell out. If they don't sell out, I don't cover my money.

It's Tuesday night which means it's salsa dancing for Ma and Da. Da hates it but it keeps Ma happy and if he's learnt anything in twenty-one years of marriage it's that things are better when Mum's happy.

It also means that I've got to get dinner. I'm going to walk into town and get three baguettes from Michelle. Michelle works five days a week from Monday to Saturday and she has Wednesday off. I never go on Wednesday.

On the way through town Mrs O'Dowd spots me and scuttles across the road to thank me for playing the Take That song earlier on. She pats me on the upper arm, before rubbing me like a horse, then scuttling back across the road. Apparently when the songs come on she stops everyone in the shop from doing anything and turns the music up so she can listen to her boys sing.

I walk through the supermarket to Michelle's counter at the back. She sees me coming and does a little baby wave thing that girls do. My face goes red as I pull a beamer. I thought I'd stopped that happening. I'm a hormonal teenage boy so my body being under my own control and me looking smooth are not options available at present. One day I'm hoping it'll calm down and I could look the slightest bit cool, but it's not happening today. She looks a delight today as ever.

'Now what can I get you, young Mister Lex?' she says through a smile. She definitely likes me, I'm sure she does. More likely she definitely knows I like her; she'd be a fool not to. She's probably just being sweet to me, so as to let me down gently. I'm not an eejit.

I wonder what she'd say if I just came out with, 'How's about you dump that arsebiscuit of a boyfriend of yours?' Why do women go for such arseholes? I never understand that. She's always defending him to her friends; they think he's an arsehole too.

'Can I have two roast beef sandwiches with salad and mayonnaise and one salad sandwich with no mayonnaise and no butter for me sister.'

My sister Fiona has gone veggie; she won't even eat fish. She's a moron; we live in the west of Ireland with beautiful cows and beautiful fish. She's such a fool; it's like taking a deaf person to a gig. Anyway there's nothing we can do with her and we've tried. I told her that in return for the animals getting to live somewhere so beautiful as the west coast of Ireland we get to eat them, it's a fair deal. God brokered it himself.

Michelle makes the sandwiches with her hands, which incidentally are lovely – all of her is lovely. She looks up to catch me staring at her, and she giggles to herself and finishes off the two roast beef. To be fair, it's not just me who loves her; everyone loves her. Sometimes at lunch on Saturday she'll have three guys queuing for her to make their sandwiches while the others behind the counter are free. It must piss Liam off no end, which is a good thing.

I'm going to play Dr Hook, 'When You're in Love with a Beautiful Woman' tomorrow. I should write that down.

I have an idea as I'm walking out of the supermarket carrying the sandwiches. At the festival I could have a Miss Clifden competition. She could win it; she'd walk it and I could kiss her on stage in front of everyone, on the lips. That would piss Liam off, which is good. I'll write that down too.

I get back home just as drizzle is starting to come down. Fiona is downstairs rotting her brain with a soap opera; Sean is upstairs on his PS2. We eat the sandwiches together around the kitchen table, and then they go back to what they were doing. None of us talk during the meal.

I go upstairs to do a bit of my homework revision. Tomorrow is my last English class ever before the study leave. I quite like our teacher, Mr Hickey; he likes to create arguments, or debates as he calls them, in the class. He's a good guy for someone who cares so much about sport. I'm lucky he's not going to be marking my papers; he'll give you an extra mark if you're one of the sporty lads, which I'm not.

School's OK for me; I've never really minded it. Davey always thought of it as more akin to a prison camp and talked about tunnelling out to freedom. That's why he left at sixteen after the Junior Cert, which was a shame as, although he was in different streams to me, it meant I had someone to hang out with on the breaks. Not that I get a chance to hang out much these days, with the station and all.

I'm hoping LSE will be different. I like learning new things, but I worry it will be super-hard and above my head. At least I won't have to ever learn about bloody Marconi again. At school, just so you know my place, I'm like not one of the really cool popular ones because I'm rubbish at sport, in fact I don't like sport at all. You know there's that book *The God Delusion* that everyone is going on about and that guy saying it's all rubbish and what they believe in is rubbish; why don't they do one called *The Sport Delusion*, to challenge all these rabidly devoted people who believe in something that is essentially futile and pointless and achieves nothing? All it does is distract you for two days on the weekend from the fact that your job is fucking boring and going nowhere and that your wife is a fat miserable old bag who's let herself go. I should write that down, I'm having some good ideas today.

Anyway so I'm not like one of the sporty ones, and I suppose I am one of the clever ones, so I'm bright but not the brightest, and I think I get a little bit more kudos because of the radio station.

Like I'm not as clever as Niall Regan, but then I'm also not a total sack like him.

So I'm sort of one of the middle ones cool-wise, but slightly elevated, does that make sense? Like I'm crap at sport making me not cool, and I'm a bit too clever to be cool, but then I've got the station and people think that's cool, so that gets me up a notch.

So I started up a radio station: I love music and I want to be a radio DJ one day. I don't have the skill to be a musician, I don't think I could make it as a singer; I don't have the balls to go out there. I could play bass, that's about the height of my stage presence; haven't got the energy for drums, the talent for lead guitar, the charisma for lead singer. I know where my place would be. Bass, producer or Svengali. I would make a good Svengali but I don't have the clothes and I think Svengalis have to be evil; you never hear of a nice Svengali. I could be the first nice Svengali.

Failing those I could be a radio DJ, get into all the best gigs, get to hang out with bands. When I go to London I'm definitely going to try to get in a band, just to be in one to see what it's like and to fail gloriously but I'm going to give it a go. So like when bands come into the studio and I have to interview them I can nod and say, 'Yeah I used to play in venues like that, isn't that dressing room disgusting,' giving me a kind of kinship with them: I've walked in your shoes. Man.

2

So I started up a radio station: illegal, pirate, underground, bedroom, hobby, those are all the names that get used for these types of get-ups. I prefer the term 'neighbourhood' as it is local, made for the people of Clifden by the people of Clifden, or by a person in Clifden.

The Internet was a great source of information; that's where I found out how to set the station up. Obviously I've got a good starting point, in that I've got loads and loads of music on my computer already. I got most of it when file sharing wasn't as cracked down upon as it is now. All my stuff now is secure and I don't sign up to any file-sharing networks any more, as that's how they hammer you. I know they got this guy who had like 20,000 tracks on his set-up. I've got 5,000 so I reckon I'd be on their radar for definite, if I were to keep at it.

So I've got a good starting point. I stuck loads of extra memory onto my PC so it can cope with all the files, and it's a pretty quick Dell with Intel Pentium processor.

Next part was the mixing desk, so I can open up the

mic and speak into it then fade it down and the music back up. I bought this second-hand off eBay from a guy in Birmingham, England. The day it came I nearly pissed me leg. It's beautiful. I'd carry a picture of it in my wallet if I were sure no one would find out. I had the model picture of it as a screen saver for a while, even though the bugger was sat in front of me.

The only problem with setting a playlist running is the tracks go one into another, so if a song has a long boring beginning or takes a while to finish it's kind of like dead air which you wouldn't have on a proper station. So you could never play the Stone Roses' 'I Wanna Be Adored', cos it has got two minutes of nothing and muffled music at the beginning. Usually a professional DJ would talk over that stuff but as I'm not here for 80 per cent of the time I just have to let them run into one another.

The mixing desk I bought was thanks to the money I made setting up websites for people. I'm pretty much the only guy in town for doing stuff like that. Clifden is about 2,000 people and I'm the only one in the area who knows how to set up a website and who knows how to do it halfway decently. I'm not that good neither, especially when you see some of the sites out there. The thing was I could do it, I didn't cost too much and there was a sudden rush of people asking for them: the hotel, the restaurants, the pubs all needed them. Tourists would ask if they had a web page when they phoned up or visited, so they found out who did their neighbour's website and it all came back to me.

I just do a basic-stuff home page plus five or six offshoot pages, and with a few questions to tailor it for them and some pictures, a bit of narrative and a contact email address, I was able to knock them out at €600 a pop. Not bad for an afternoon's work. I made them think it took me a week though, so they thought they were getting value for money.

I'll admit that I am a bit of a geek; I like the minutiae of life that builds up to bigger things. I was always interested in taking things apart and putting them back together, like CD players, to see how they worked, and to look at the circuit boards on computers: they fascinated me. I've just got to know how it works. I would love to take a telly apart, can you imagine how clever you must have to be to understand how a telly works and how all the parts link together, let alone to be the person to invent it in the first place. I wonder if people are only so clever for one part of the TV, like the chips and circuit boards, and someone else is clever for another part. I wonder if someone knows how every piece of a plane works or one guy is the engine guy and one guy is the electronics and one guy is the wings and hydraulics. Man, sometimes there's just too much stuff to know. I'm never going to know it all. It's like that Ian Dury song, 'There Ain't Half Been Some Clever Bastards'.

So anyway I just used the same template on everyone's set-up, €600 in cash and www.Bob.ie is your uncle. Most of the computer and radio equipment is paid for out of that money. I've got some saved up for when college starts but it has also meant I haven't had to get a part-time job over the summer, which is sweet as I'm pretty crap at dealing with the tourists and that's all the summer work there is around here.

This town isn't the most embracing towards the advance of the Internet but there are a few real surprises. Because of the setting-up websites stuff and all, I would often get asked general computer stuff by people who know what I can do but I don't even know them. I was the town's unofficial IT department for a while. Like Percy Milne, an old English guy who retired here, he must be eighty-odd, and he got a computer delivered so he can link up to see his daughter in Australia and his grandsons. I had to go round his house to set it up for him and write down the instructions and tape it to the table. I did that one for free; he's a nice old guy. His house smells of death since his wife passed away but he's sound. I put the child protection filter on his computer, so he didn't have to see any unwanted images. I don't want him to have a heart attack and it all be my fault because I hadn't protected him from the filth out there. I'm not having that on my conscience.

Imagine having to explain that to his daughter at the funeral: 'I'm so sorry for your troubles . . . yes you're right, it was me who unfortunately discovered his body; his face was frozen in shock as lesbian nymphets wrestled in chip fat across the monitor screen . . . I like to think he died happy, if somewhat shocked.'

Anyway someone had told someone, who had told him

that I was the guy to talk to for all the web-Internet stuff. It's not that I'm that much cop at it, it's just no one else can really do it, hence cleaning up when it came to setting up websites for some of the businesses in town.

So I got the music, got the mixing desk; all I needed was to be able to transmit it. The transmitter cost me €600 but came with an aerial and all leads. It cost €70 to get it shipped over from London and I can't tell you how I got it, but it was hard to get and I managed it.

As we're on the hillside that looks out over the town we've got a pretty good starting point as a place to broadcast from. We slipped the window cleaner €20 to climb up the ladder and attach it to our telly aerial.

I went through all the frequencies a decimal point at a time to make sure I was not over anything else and well away from the services. Eventually I settled on 106.5 FM and stuck it on with a test signal.

It took a bit of dicking about with to get a proper clear signal but when I did finally I went proper mental, it was so super-cool. Da was the only one who knew at the start as I had to ask him in order to get the window cleaner up there. He said he didn't tell Mum as she's not the most receptive to things like this, being perpetually worried about 'our good name'.

I got into the Maytals when I was fourteen. I was in Zhivago Records and looking for a reggae album. I'd never owned one before, never listened to one and I thought I should check it out, maybe learn a bit. I was going through the racks and I saw this black and white chessboard-like cover and it was called 20 Reggae Classics Volume 2 *for €4. I got it home and stuck it on. The first track was '54–46 Was My Number' and I was blown away; it was totally awesome. There's another Maytals track on it too called 'Pomps and Pride' and it's the second best track on the whole thing, after '54–46'. So I got on Amazon looking for Volume 1, as if this is Volume 2 then what's the first one like? I find it and I order it straight away. Then I spent the rest of the day trying to rip all the Maytals tunes I can off LimeWire.*

That album changed my life I tell you, changed it forever.

I'm the only guy in this town who can speak to the whole town and that gives me a certain position of power. I could spread rumours and they would travel faster than any other way. Well actually they would only just about be faster than the rumour mill in this town, as that is lightning.

I could throw up outside the pub and Ma could know about it before I'm home. She'll certainly know it by next morning.

Or if I swear on the radio, Ma always finds out about it. I'm bad in that I swear a bit too much in real life and it's a massive no-no on professional radio, so I need to cut that out. I really beat myself up about it when one does slip out, especially when you think of who listens to me.

I shouldn't need to swear on the radio; I should have a

big enough and quick enough vocab to get me out of that situation. I need a kind of inbuilt alarm that will stop it from ever coming out.

Just like with callers-in; that's so much harder to do than you'd think, just chatting to people and making sure they don't do anything. Kids are the worst, especially the young lads; they are always trying to do it. I love it when they are just building up to a swear and I can sense it in their voice and I cut them off just before they do it, or fade them down, then I can hear it in my ear but know it didn't go out. Then I give them a bollocking, tell them I'm going to speak to their folks, listen to them shite themselves and apologise, then I tell them to feck off.

3

FIONA

I love Lex. It's my secret. I should love him, he's my brother, but he thinks I don't even like him but I love him. Sometimes I see him smiling at me and he says he can tell what I'm thinking. I know he can't; he's clever but not that clever.

Lex does very well at school, and Mummy is really proud of him and hopes that he will go to university. He's got his big exams coming up and I think he will be OK, but he's very worried about them. That's why we have to tiptoe round the house if it is study time for him: everybody has to be quiet for him if Lex is working.

I am not too loud around the house. The main person who gets shouted at for noise is Sean as he won't stop banging things or kicking balls against the walls.

I don't like the music Lex likes. He tries to make me like it and if I put something on downstairs that I like he will make me turn it off. He seems to think only the music that he likes is good and everything else is rubbish. Different people can like different things but Lex doesn't seem to understand that.

Lex always says if I go in his room he will burn my magazines. I still go in though as I know he won't catch me. Sean saw me go in and said that he would tell Lex so I told him to come in as well and now he can't tell Lex as he will get in trouble too.

I don't want him to go away to university and definitely not to London anyway, as I like him being around. London is too far away, he should have chosen Dublin as that way we could still go see him.

Also he won't be here to protect me especially when I go to the big school. I'm not looking forward to that at all.

And I don't want him to go to London because I am worried he won't be safe. He's tall, but he's not very strong so I worry for him. London is going to be much rougher than here. I hope he will be OK. I hope they will be nice to him; apparently they are very rude.

I think Lex will be famous someday. He wants to be a radio DJ. All the girls at school ask about Lex; they think he's amazing. Mary goes on and on about him; it's so embarrassing. She is my best friend but it's gross: how would she like it if all I would talk about was her brother? As if I would.

Mary is a vegetarian too; we both decided to become vegetarian together. We watched a programme on what they do to the animals and I just felt sick.

Lex is a good big brother though; he's not a toughie but

he's clever and if I asked him for help he would help me. He likes to try and help me with my schoolwork but I don't need him as I can do it all by myself. We started to get homework from school so we would be ready for the big school, as you get homework there. He talks to me as if I'm really stupid sometimes but I understand it; it's not that hard.

It might be harder for boys. I read in a magazine that girls develop quicker than boys, so although the girls are in the same year as the boys I think maybe we should be a year ahead or they a year behind. It's not their fault, they just make them that way. And besides they just play football all the time and anyway they wouldn't notice.

Lex doesn't play football: he says he doesn't like it. I think it's because he's not very good at it. He's not very coordinated when it comes to sporty things. When we were on holiday in France we played rackets on the beach. He was playing Daddy and he kept missing the ball so he just got really angry and stormed off up the beach. Lex does sometimes get angry; not very often, usually if he thinks people are not listening to him. He thinks everything he says is so important and it's not. If you talk over him or ignore him that's what makes him shout the most. Sometimes I do that to make him angry if he's been nasty to me.

He is in love, which is really sad, as the girl he is in love with doesn't love him. I don't know if she knows he's in love with her. When we go into Super-Value he makes Sean and me wait outside but we don't; we sneak down the side and we watch him when he goes and speaks to her. His hands are always shaking but he tries to keep them down by his side so she can't see them.

I don't think she will go out with Lex; she is very pretty and very nice but she is going out with a bigger boy called Liam who is much tougher and better-looking than Lex. I think he is an Alpha Male. An Alpha Male is the biggest and the strongest and the best girls go for them like animals do.

She is pretty though; she is good enough for Lex and I think he is good enough for her. He is clever too: he would make her happy but she is older and older girls don't go out with younger boys unless the younger boy is really, really cool and also I think she is happy with her boyfriend.

Lex doesn't get many girls. He's not ugly and I think girls do like him. Maybe if he got his hair cut to be more stylish: it's all like a quiff and I think it would look better if he got it cut. I told him before I would give him a style makeover and make him look better. I think he will get a girl in London. I've never been to London; I would like to go. I would have to go with Mummy and Daddy first as I am not old enough to go on my own.

I really hope his concert thing goes OK for Lex: it makes him so worried and that's when he gets angry and shouts at me. I know he doesn't mean it, as on the whole Lex is a nice person. I asked him if our dance troupe could do a dance at the show and he said no it was not that kind of show but I think it could be great.

If the show is good everyone will think Lex is the best. Mummy and Daddy think he's the best already; they say they love us all the same but they really like Lex the most. They smile at each other when he goes out the door sometimes then they kiss which is super-gross.

If I had to describe Lex in three words I would say Clever, Nice, Selfish.

4

My friend Davey is not a well fella: he's not well in the head. Like physically this is his hometown; mentally I don't know what planet he lives on. He's a guy you either like or avoid, so most people avoid him because they don't get him. I don't get him either but it's a top craic hanging around with him and that's good enough for me.

He doesn't have too many mates other than me, which makes me worry for him when I go away. I don't want him to progress to being the town idiot; it's a very possible career destination for him, and I'm surprised our jobs advisor didn't pull that one out and suggest it the last time they visited. When he was still at school he was the lunatic of our year. Not 'nutter' as in dangerous or nasty-heading-for-prison nutter, but he's such a random and people who are randoms make other people nervous. This could lead to him getting picked on, especially by those in the years above who'd go for anyone who stood out because they're dickheads.

The thing with Davey is he doesn't back down. A bit of

it is natural stupidity but he also has this thing and if, and it's a big fucking if, there was ever any inner logic to Davey it was always, 'I did it to see what would happen.'

It'll be on his gravestone, 'His last words were: "I'm gonna bite into this electric cable to see what will happen."'

I remember this one time on the path between the third and fourth year playgrounds that goes round the back of the science room, and Aaron Connor is coming the other way and Me and Davey are just minding our own and trying to walk down one side of the path. Then Connor steps on the other side to block us so we simply switch sides and he does it again. I should mention here that Aaron Connor is an ape; I think he went through puberty at about nine and hasn't stopped growing. Apparently he has to shave at lunchtime to stop him growing a beard by tea.

So Aaron starts having a go at Davey, starts calling him a feckin loon and special needs, and he's bearing down on him and stuff. And then Davey just wallops him. He wallops him as hard as I've ever seen Davey wallop anything; it lands between Connor's chin and neck and it does nothing. Connor's face goes scarlet with anger at what Davey's done and then he starts hammering these punches on Davey who's got himself covered up with his arms, and me and some others are trying to pull Connor off of him. Eventually a teacher came and split it up, and sent us to the headmistress's office.

After we got our bollocking and detentions and were walking home I said to Davey, 'What the bloody hell did you do that for? He's a monster for Christ's sake, there was no way you were going to win against him, even if you had a bloody army.' Davey responded by saying, 'I know, I just wanted to see what would happen if I smacked him one. He was shouting at me and I couldn't stop thinking, "What would happen if I hit him?" Next thing you know I just couldn't *not* hit him; I had to hit him, so I hit him.'

Two weeks' detention for that; mine got suspended so as not to go on my permanent school record. They give me these little privileges sometimes: it's a bit unfair on Davey but if you are getting the good grades then they can let you off little bits cos the better the grades you get the better it reflects on the school for their results. Davey was never going to get the grades so they don't let things slide with him. That said, it was all his fault in the first place so I don't feel too bad about it.

OK, so another example of him was last night, and this is pure Davey, classic unrefined stupidity. Me, Davey, Danny and Danny's brother Stephen were all drinking at the Harp; we've got our table which is just in on your right-hand side as you come into the old man's bar bit, and we're having a good night and all. Danny's brother Stephen is only sixteen and it's one of the first times he's been out drinking with us, and he's stocious after about two pints. We're telling him all this bullshit about if you're found being drunk on the streets and you're not with a woman then you're a single drinker and a potential drunkard so then the Gardi can throw you in the back of the van, give you a hiding and stick you in the cells for the night and there's nothing you can do about it. The Gardi like to think of it as training and do it to keep 'match fit'.

We're telling him that that's why everyone tries to score with a woman at last orders, otherwise if they get caught solo on their walk home they're taking serious chances. And if you can't score with them then you have to at least try to walk them home so it looks like you're with someone; y'know that's why guys say, 'Can I walk you home?' Stephen is lapping this shit up, 'You're joking, no way?' and we're like, 'For real.'

Eventually Danny says he's going to be staying over at mine tonight and that Stephen is going to have to walk back alone so he better try to get himself a woman to walk home or he's for it.

It's last orders and we egg Stephen on to go up to the bar and try to get a woman to go home with him. We tell him as he's a novice we'll let him go first and we'll try afterwards. He goes up to this woman and she's like definitely over forty, so could easily have been his mum. She's got this shitey leather jacket and that tight-screw bubble perm thing going on with some red in it, though it could be the light she's standing under. She's checking her face in the mirror behind the bar when Stephen approaches and says something; she looks over and me, Danny and Davey are roaring with laughter, absolutely wetting ourselves.

The woman doesn't quite hear what Stephen's said; she thinks he's taking the piss out of her and that's why we're laughing so much. It turns out she's with a fella and he looks a right shifty bastard. She tells him that the boy and us were taking the piss out of her, at which point Michael, the landlord, spies what's going on, comes over to us and tells us to drink up and it's time to go.

We get outside and Stephen's all 'What? What? What?', but we're still creasing up.

As we get outside the pub, in the middle of the square where all the cars are parked there's only an actual paddy wagon that they use for all the riots and stuff. I grab Stephen and go, 'Holy shit man, that's the van they use, that's the one that's going to pick you up and do you if you don't get home quickly, you better leg it.'

At this point Davey sprints off round the corner, no 'see ya' or anything, just turns and runs away. None of us know why, and we continue ribbing Stephen until he cottons on eventually that it's one big wind-up.

Stephen starts giving it I knew all along and he was just playing along for the craic. At least that's what he's trying to say, but his words miss '. . . wrong . . . stop . . . naaaaahhh, I knew I knew . . . not thick . . .' as they fall out of his mouth in random order.

Danny realises Stephen is starting to be a bit of a mess, so gathers him up and sticks his arm around him, like a boxing coach whose boy has taken enough of a beating in the ring and can't continue. Stephen protests but knows his brother is right, and the protest is a weak one.

We're about to set off when out of nowhere Davey comes running down the middle of the road. He's coming round the corner and he's going flat out, proper hundred metres style, arms pumping, absolutely sprinting for his life. My first thought is that someone is chasing him but they're not. As he comes round the corner he sets his sights on the Garda van: he's got another forty yards to go and he's hurtling towards it at full pace. He keeps running. Ten yards left: then five yards before it he leaps off his left foot, turns his shoulder in towards it and hits the side panels of it as hard as he can.

There's this huge bang as he hits it, like a massive 'DANK!' The guys inside the van are shat up; Davey hits the ground and is rolling around in agony and letting out this awful moan of a sound. He pulls himself up and limps off in another direction and he's gone, with the two guards scrambling out the van, fucked off and now rared up to sort someone out. They then start walking briskly into the darkness after Davey.

I mean why would anyone do something like that? It's just not right.

And that's Davey.

It's not right.

But it is very funny.

And I don't understand it. But he's my best mate so I suppose I don't need to.

Anyway there's like four of us in our lot, like our minigang, but we're not nearly retarded enough to ever refer to it as a gang. There's Davey and me then there's Danny and Doh. Doh is short for David Doherty but everyone just calls him Doh: even his mum calls him Doh, which is a bit weird. And like out of the four of us it's really me and Davey who are best mates, and Danny and Doh are much closer to each other that they are to us, but we all knock about together.

But it's more like I'm mates with Danny and Doh; Davey wouldn't really go out with them independently.

At school we just sort of ended up hanging out together at the same spot. We were sort of the non-sporty ones, but not the geeky ones; it's not even like we're totally non-sporty. Davey is well into playing sports but people got tired of his overeagerness and he'd get too excited and someone would end up hurt and in the end they stopped asking him to play footy at lunchtime until he got the message.

As I said before, sport and me we're not so good together; the whole sport and winners thing just doesn't work for me.

Winners are fucking losers anyway man, the whole notion of winning is for losers, and I'm not just saying this because of the sport thing and me not being good at it; they're fucking losers for real.

For a start winners are almost always tools: that single-mindedness, to be so focused on something that it obsesses your entire being, just makes you into a tool.

And because there's so much bloody sport on TV and everything, these dull bastards get a platform to spout their rubbish about being winners and how important winning is.

Look at the bloody Olympics. I bet if you found the biggest

country that had the lowest percentage of winners in relation to size you'd probably find the soundest country.

We Irish don't go in for that winning shite if we can help it.

Look at like Holland and France: they don't bother winning stuff. If they do it's in a really cool way like Cruyff and that and even then they didn't win. And they're a sound nation, and the French, they don't win stuff, not the indigenous French; the north Africans and people from their foreign colonies they win stuff for them, but the French, they are smoking Gauloises, drinking wine and eating cheese; they are not worried about being the best physically: that's for idiots.

So rugby, we are all right as a nation at rugby, and I don't mind rugby as a sport for two reasons. One, it's basically an excuse to go drinking together with a big group of mates, and I can see the logic in that: you go out and do something unpleasant and are bonded by doing it together, and you celebrate that bond by getting hammered together. It's a bit homo and that but I get it. The other reason why I like it is it's big blokes hurting each other, and I figure if they are hurting each other then there's less chance of them hurting me; the game is just stupid donkeys hurting themselves.

The one thing I totally don't understand though, and I don't know if I am the only person who ever thought this about sport or whether other people have this opinion, but our voice is just suppressed like in Iran or something, by parties with a vested interest in keeping us down. In fact I don't know if this opinion scares them too much because the whole house of cards that is sport would be brought to the ground if someone pointed this out, just like saying the Emperor isn't wearing any clothes, but here it goes: At international level and even lower, you're thirty massive guys dedicating your lives, your efforts and your entire beings into fighting it out for what? For fucking what? For a fucking peanut-shaped ball. I mean who fucking cares who has got it; honestly, what are you going to do when you get it? Run over there, so what? Really so what, but not just rugby, all sport. Golf – I'm going to hit that ball into that hole. Football – we're going to kick that ball into that net. So?

Sport lays waste to millions of lives in the pursuit of something entirely pointless. I'm not saying getting fit isn't good for you and of course there's the camaraderie, but the action of it all is so pointless. In fact that's the biggest irony of all; they battle it out for points and it's all so fucking pointless. I'll write that one down.

At our school there was this lad called Jerry Wilson and he was brilliant at sport, like brilliant at football and brilliant at running and at basketball and everything, and in games we'd just give the ball to him to let him go and be brilliant, and everyone thought he was like the Johnny Bollocks. But like, if you ever talked to him, man he was boring. I used to like to try to talk to him to see if I could keep the topic off sport and he wouldn't know he was doing it but he'd always try to make the conversation about sport even when it wasn't, so if you could keep him off it it was like torture to him; he'd desperately want to get back to safe ground.

But like, why do people spend all this time trying to be the best at sport; why do people not strive to be the most interesting. Interesting is better than good at sport, and I don't mean the cleverest: there's plenty of stuff for clever. Clever doesn't mean interesting, although interesting people are usually clever.

Jesus, don't ever get me started on horse racing. Oh my life, in the entire history of mankind has ever so much effort and money gone into doing something so utterly idiotic? So you're telling me you've dedicated your whole life to a sport that is based on finding if one horse is faster than another? Really? Shall we see which cow is best at the long jump next? Jokers the lot of 'em.

The funny thing is, one of my pet joys, and it's like a real guilty pleasure, which I don't know why I do it, but I always like reading interviews with sports stars. They fascinate me, just because maybe it's a snobby thing but I just enjoy it when they sound really dull and boring; maybe it's some cheap trick to make me feel better about myself. I am curious seeing them and trying to understand them, like how they're wired to do that and be like that.

For me it's like, enjoy the trophies and medals you got in your twenties as you've got a lot of your life for them to keep you company while you bore yourself to your death in old age.

That's probably wrong isn't it? Boring people probably don't get bored because they are boring so have a lower interest bar. Interesting people get bored easier. Peter Cook, I read a biography about him, he was really interesting but he was really bored; it's why he drank.

To be interesting and keep being interesting and keep being interested, that is the pinnacle that's the ultimate goal of man, not to climb a fucking mountain or score a fucking goal.

That's what I've got to do if I get into radio; I'm going to have to be interesting for people, interesting enough for them to want to listen to me, interested enough in music to be able to know a lot of great tunes (I know full well if I'm going to do it professionally I'm going to have to play a lot of records I don't like, but I'm willing to sacrifice that to slide in the ones I do and make a difference where I can).

I can see the benefits of sport: the camaraderie, the friendship and the fitness and I totally understand those and appreciate those and I'm not trying to eliminate those, and that's just like the atheists saying there's no God and that what you believe in is rubbish but the benefits to society of religions and the benefits to the community we still appreciate. So what I'm saying is two points, three points, five points, ten points: these points that you are battling for, they don't actually exist; someone just made them up to make you fight for them. Am I the only one who can see it; is no one else aware or just too afraid to say the unsayable, that this is all just made-up rubbish, and a monstrous waste of time.

At school they've all got their English teams and it's

always Man U or Liverpool and they're fighting it out for three points: three points of what? Three made-up points, that's what. To win a made-up league, for a trophy which represents you got the most made-up points in the made-up league.

Morons.

I suppose the big reason people don't mention these facts is the fear of the void it would create if ever this illusion was destroyed. 'Now what?' is what they'd say. Men would stand in silence in pubs staring blankly at one another.

Danny likes sport too and he's not bad but the rest of us didn't bother so he stopped bothering.

Out of the four of us Doh is a clever one too. I'm not saying there's a correlation between people who like sport being thick and people who don't being clever, because that's not true, there's plenty of people who like sport who are clever; all I'm saying is that there's not many thick people who don't like sport.

And also I'm not saying Danny and Davey are stupid cos they're not. Davey is not of a species that is measurable by exams, so it's not fair to judge him that way, and Danny is reasonably clever but just not in Doh's league.

The hard thing for Danny must be that he works really hard to be averagely clever, whereas Doh has got to be the single laziest person I have ever met in my life; I mean lazy to the point of atrophy. I swear to God when he dreams, he dreams of being asleep. And he's incredibly lazy but still really bright; if he actually bothered to try he could be way brainier than me, but he just doesn't want to. And he's going to waste it, any talent or brains that he's got he is going to waste, and it's not that you can feel sorry for him yet because he hasn't wasted it yet but he's going to, and someone ought to tell him, but he's not going to listen to any of us.

Like at school if you'd ask his exam result and he'd pull the same face after telling you whether he got an A or a D and the face was as if he'd only filled in facetious answers to the questions anyway, so why did they bother giving me the marks?

Doh's funny though, really dry, too dry, like sometimes it's only the next day that you'd work out he was taking the piss out of you.

The one thing Doh likes to do though is lie, but not like a little white lie, or a big believable lie, just a lie of such whopping proportions that it would make you think why bother?

He once told us he had an uncle who was a whale and could only eat krill, and he was so insistent about it we just gave up and agreed.

Danny and Doh live next door to each other; they were born two weeks apart and have been friends ever since. Danny really looks up to Doh. When Doh's being funny sometimes Danny has this look of pride about him that says, 'That's my best friend.'

Danny is quieter than Doh; he doesn't hide in his shadow, but he's happier not making too much noise. He's a really good guy though, like no one has got anything bad to say about him, mainly because there isn't anything bad to him: he's just a nice quiet guy. Actually out of the four of us he's probably the most decent; he's not lazy like Doh, nuts like Davey or neurotically self-centred like me. He's probably going to be the stealthy success, and when he is I'm going to coast on his tails.

Sometimes I wish I was a bit quieter like Danny. Maybe the radio station is one big peacock tail to attract attention to myself. I hope not, as I hope there is more to me than that and I'm not that obvious. God I think I'm going to end up with a shrink someday as if I ever ended up telling all this to a friend or girlfriend or something then they'd just get bored, fucked off and leave me to wallow in it.

None of the four of us physically is that big, which is a shame as if we had any foresight in putting a little gang together it might have been good to have someone of reasonable size in it so as to menace anyone off. Rapier wit and a knowledge of old reggae records is no match for a beered-up culchie with a desire to kick someone's teeth in.

I doubt I'll see that much of Danny and Doh when I leave; obviously I'll see them when I come back if they're still here, but I'm not tight enough with them that I'd imagine that they'd come over and visit.

I don't know what the pair of them are going to do at the end of the summer. There was talk of them going travelling together but I don't think either of them has planned it enough to save up some money to do it.

Doh could easily go off to college but he hasn't filled

out any of the forms. He could go through the second round of offers if he changes his mind I suppose.

Frederick 'Toots' Hibbert was born in December 1945 in Maypen, Jamaica but moved to Kingston at the age of thirteen. He grew up singing gospel music in the church choir and it's a huge influence on his upbeat vocals, which have been compared to Otis Redding in their raspy soulfulness.

5

So this is the plan for the summer: I do the exams, that is the biggy and the one that is scaring me. Not that my whole life depends on them or anything but realistically it does, so they're worth worrying about.

Points-wise I need to get two A1s and an A2 or B1 to get to the London School of Economics (LSE). I looked at UCD – Dublin – and Leeds, but LSE was by far my favourite, mainly because it was in the middle of London and I know that's where I want to be, plus it's got its own student radio station called Pulse that I definitely want to get involved with.

Anyway I'll do the exams, try not to feck them up, and then work on the festival for the rest of the summer. I've got loads to do on that one and I've just not had the time as the exams have to come first.

So I will get the results, and hopefully get confirmed into LSE, then the final push for the festival and all the shite that will go with it. Hopefully successfully manage the festival and then I'm gone, I'm out of this town. I can't wait. I don't think I've outgrown it, I'm not that much of a bighead, but to be honest I'm a bit sick of the place and I'm ready for something new, if you know what I mean.

It worries me when half the town knows you, and it's not like I'm special or anything, they just know everyone. I tell you it's not good when you wake up and you know you did something wrong last night and the people you pass on the street are more likely to know than you are.

I wonder if the social grapevine will be replaced by an Internet message board in the future, where you can just get an update on everyone and what they are up to. At the moment it's just done through chat, but it can't be too long.

So it's basically the biggest, hardest point in my life so far and I've decided to make it harder by having the pressure of putting a bloody festival on because I'm a fool.

A ride would be good before I leave too, only there are not that many realistic options out there. I'm friends with a girl called Kelly who's in our sixth year, she's smart and funny but it wouldn't be right and she is too smart and decent a person to do it to. You see that's my problem; I don't want to do it with someone who is stupid and would do it with anyone but I also don't want to do it with someone who's smart enough to know that the only reason I'm doing it with them is to get it done.

At least with Michelle I would be doing it because I really, really, desperately wanted to. I'm like one of those once-a-decade planetary phenomena where my heart, my mind and my balls are all in perfect alignment. But she's in another galaxy.

6

So why Michelle?

Why throw all my hopes and dreams on her? The short answer is that I'm just an eejit; the long answer is the same but with some justification as to why I'm an eejit.

As I said before, Lex won't do shabby, and he won't do talking in the third person either, that stops here; I'm not that much of a pretentious arse. I'm not saying I'm a snob or anything but I'm saying that if I'm going to fall for a girl she's going to be good. We're a small pool in Clifden; the choice isn't that spectacular, but I am painfully aware that I am giving myself a crazy challenge by choosing someone like her.

My sister reckons that I purely like her as she is unattainable and that I am testing out my feelings of love against something I can't possibly get and thus protecting myself from ever truly being heartbroken. She said it is very similar to young girls and their crushes on boy band members, who they love with all their hearts but know they can't have; thus when the decision comes for the love to end it's the girl letting go of her feelings of love rather than being truly rejected. Eleven, she's fecking eleven years old for Christ's sake and she's coming out with shite like that. Her and her friends read all those magazines for girls who are supposed to be about ten years older than them. I found her looking at handbags the other day; I mean Jesus what does she need with a fecking handbag, all she does is go to school each day. She's growing up far too quickly: I'm going to have to keep a real eye on her. She called me a narcissist the other day and she's ELEVEN.

I don't like the fact that she bloody knows anyway. The whole family bloody knows: it's openly discussed at the dinner table; it's humiliating, my failure to get Michelle to like me is standard kitchen table talk. Ma will ask if I've seen her recently, to which Da will give me some useless advice which is more than likely to be about how he won her heart (since we're on the topic, it was by staring at her; he gave her the old 'Donal stare'. It's a yarn that's been spun so many times that the walls sigh with resignation when it looks like he's about to unravel it again.)

I don't know what the answer is. I mean I'm seventeen and I know my biology and I know I should be after anything that walks with a wiggle but I'm not. I wonder if something is the matter with me. If this time of my life is supposed to be my sexual peak then it's a pretty low peak. And it's not really sexual either, I just really like her. I don't want to say love as I'm old enough to know that it's not love until it's like proper-proper but I know I can't stop thinking about her and I feel that I might be sick whenever I see her.

So anyway, why her? I don't know, she's not particularly cool or anything; from what I know about her she doesn't know too much about music. If I'm going to marry a girl one day then she has to be cool and like music, I mean proper music. I'm never going to find a girl like that in this town.

So why? She's just beautiful, like really, really beautiful. She's the most beautiful girl in this town, no question. And she isn't old enough to know it too much yet. She does know it; she'd have to be bloody stupid for her not to know it but she hasn't let it go to her head. And she doesn't know it so much that she's become professional at dealing with it. Besides her beauty rarely gets her into trouble as she has the rolling menace of Liam to scare the shit out of anyone foolish enough to think they might have a chance. I mean they'd have to be an absolute fool to think they had a shot at her. (*a*) He'd end you; and (*b*) even if you can deal with being killed you'd then still have to woo her. Or the other way round: (*a*) you'd have to somehow woo her and she's beautiful so you haven't got a chance; and (*b*) after you wooed her he'd kill you, so you wouldn't get a chance to enjoy it as you're now dead.

This is a poor starting point for any relationship. Actually I say relationship: I think I'd settle for a feel; I'd die happy with just a feel. Maybe I could just straight out ask her: I'll stop all this leering and obsessing if you just let us have a quick feel.

And how do you go about getting yourself a girl like this? I mean there seems to be a point when they are available and from then off they'll be taken for the rest of their lives.

Liam is just that kind of shite. He's sporty, admittedly not ugly: the girls in our year used to squeak when they talked about him; I am sure they'd all sniff his jockstraps given the chance, the eejits. With Michelle's looks, I think she was one of those girls that like in a horse race is just there or thereabouts: no one really notices them and then suddenly a furlong from the end they just blossom and explode and then there they are, in the lead by far, and you wonder how could you not have noticed them before. That's probably what happened with Liam. All the girls liked him, and when Michelle suddenly became a good-looking young woman, he noticed her and that was that. Three years they've been going out. Imagine having to talk to someone as stupid as Dansey for three whole years. Christ she's probably still just waiting for him to finish his first sentence.

He got no exams leaving school; I know because I got into the school records. That and you can tell. He's going to die in this town. They'll stay together until she's about twenty-three then he'll ask her to marry him, because he'll never do any better. She'll either run then or wish she'd run a year into the marriage when they start talking about kids because she'll realise a lifetime stuck with that moron is not a lifetime worth having.

If they ever split up he'll then spend the rest of his

twenties drinking and behaving like a tool, then will get married to some second choice and will have a couple of kids, and when he can't play football any more, all that booze will catch up with him and his body will become middle-aged overnight. Then he'll get cirrhosis and they'll divorce and he'll die an alcoholic at forty-four all without ever having an original or interesting thought in his life. It's clear as day. I should warn her, leaving him now would save him.

Actually maybe that should be my campaign: rather than choose me, just don't choose him; this is the life you've got ahead of you, any dreams you have are going to be slowly muffled, and while we're about it I would be a suitable option for you to follow your dreams. Failing that could I just have a feel?

I think he is my nemesis. Maybe not my nemesis because I don't think he hates me. Maybe he does, maybe he can see I'm a threat, like a young male lion cub; actually he's not a nemesis, he's just an obstacle. He's an obstacle I need to overcome but an obstacle I've decided to start to hate. It's good to have a focus.

I did have an idea, and it was based on a story I'd heard about my grandfather. When my grandfather was young he was pretty small and wiry. His dad, so that's my great-granddad, used to knock his wife – my great-grandmother – about, so at about fourteen he started this campaign to eat double of everything he could; any opportunity he would eat extra portions if possible. He had a part-time job delivering bread and he spent some of that money back on food, and he tried to get fit too, so that he could really bulk up and so that one day he could stop his dad. That one day came pretty soon. His dad came home drunk and started pushing his mum around; granddad ran downstairs and stood in the living room and told his dad to leave her alone.

He tried to stop his dad and then granddad wrestled him to the ground and held him down to show him he was stronger. When eventually granddad let him go he tried to hit his mum. At that point granddad punched him once and knocked him out. His dad never did anything like that again.

That's another of our Donal legends. But I'm worried that if I spent six months training and eating double and getting fit and getting sharp Liam would still kick me all over town and it would be a pretty crap story to tell the grandkids.

So Michelle it is, and Michelle it will be. I try not to be too whiny about it but sometimes it does get me down.

Is this just teenage angst bollocks? Probably, but Christ I've got fuck all else to do with my hormones in this town so indulge me will you?

Toots and the Maytals were originally called The Maytals. They were formed in 1962 when Frederick 'Toots' Hibbert met Henry 'Raleigh' Gordon and Nathaniel 'Jerry' McCarthy in Kingston, Jamaica. Their style was a mixture of ska, rocksteady and reggae mixed with a soulful/gospel style of vocals. Toots was the front man of the group, with the harmony vocals of the others making up their sound.

In 1971 producer Byron Lee changed their name from 'The Maytals' to 'Toots and the Maytals'.

In 1982 Toots went solo.

In the early Nineties Toots created a new Maytals and started to tour the world.

They have had thirty-one number one hits in Jamaica.

7

With the radio station I try to just do my own voice: it's harder than you think to find a voice. Like some guys put on this fake voice, this radio voice; it's either mid-Atlantic or worse just mindlessly positive. THAT WAS A GREAT RECORD BY T'PAU AND NEXT UP A GREAT RECORD FROM LIONEL RICHIE!!!!!! It's just sickening. I try to just be me, try to do it in as natural voice as I can, maybe on air I speak a bit quicker and like a tiny bit higher, and I am less lazy with my words, but I try to come across as genuine.

Links are the talking bits between the songs, so with the station being on so much during the day and me being the only DJ, that's a lot of links for one person to do. You've got to come up with new stuff at each link and it can get really hard to be original. Sometimes I'll talk about the record; I might Wikipedia the artist during the song and just read out some facts. Other times I'll note ideas down and try to go for it. It's much harder than it sounds: you try it. Take six records and between each one come up with thirty seconds of chat that doesn't sound inane; it's a proper skill.

At least with the texts and emails you get some feedback and something to talk about and people to talk to, but sometimes you just get nothing and it feels like you're on your own.

Sometimes I just slate the records. 'That was T'Pau, my God I can't believe we actually played that; standards really are slipping round here. Next up, oh my word it's Lionel Richie: Trading Standards, take me off air, this is supposed to be a quality music show.'

That's more my style y'know, honest. If you say everything is great then nothing is great; if you say stuff is rubbish then at least when you say it's great people can believe you.

I hate U2 and I hate Bono. I've never really known why, but I think it's mainly down to the fact that they are shite and Bono is a twat; so far that is all the evidence I have.

He's Ireland's most famous person globally and he's a total knob. All I'm saying is can't we have someone not so much of an arse out there for us?

MY BEDROOM

My bedroom. I spend probably two-thirds of my life in my bedroom. I sleep in there obviously, so that's a third but a lot of the rest of my time is in there too. I do all my revising in there at my desk; the radio station is in there with the computer; I'm on the Internet a fair bit in the evenings; I hang out on a couple of forums, just posting shit and that, mainly music sites and that. I go under Clifden88, it was Cliff88 but it sounded like geriatric.

Ma constantly comes in and opens the window. She says the room smells; it doesn't but she says it does. She'll come in when the station is on and just open the window; problem is when you open the window you can hear cars from outside, although there's not that many go past as we're on an estate but when one does and the mic is open you can pick it up on the radio.

It annoys me that Ma can just walk in as well. I put a lock on the door, but Da took it off; he says there's no locks on doors in our house, apart from the bathroom. I did think of putting a red light on outside when we're on air but that's a bit wanky isn't it.

But my room, well there's a lot of black in it; the walls are black and my bed-sheets and duvet are black. It's not like I'm a goth or anything; it just looks good, and the rest of the shelves are either covered in books or CDs. I've a lot of CDs but not a lot when you consider how much music I've got backed up on my computer hard drive. If I had a CD for every track I've got on my computer this whole room would be one bloody music library.

Most of the books on the shelf are textbooks; I've got a few other books but I'm not a great reader. I know I should read more, but with the exams, the radio station and everything I don't really have the time. Maybe in London I'll read more; I know I should get some classics read like *1984* and *Brave New World* just so I know what I'm on about.

Funny thing is, in our house I haven't got the biggest room of the three of us kids which is an outrage. We used to live one road over in a three-bedroom place and I used to have to share with Sean. It was a disaster: he can't sleep properly; he like fits in his sleep. He'd wake me up through the night especially when he had nightmares. Honestly it's for the best that we moved to a four-bedroom place as if I'd've stayed sharing with Sean there'd only be two kids now; actually maybe just one as I'd be in prison.

Anyway Fiona has got a bigger room than me: only just but I measured hers against mine. Mine is 12 ft x 7 ft = 84 sq ft; hers is 11 ft x 8 ft = 88 sq ft. I should have the bigger room as I'm the oldest but she got in first when we were looking round and called it hers. Here's what I've learnt in seventeen years in our family: shout loudest – if you want something, shout loudest. You'll get it because you shouted loudest and because they want you to stop bloody shouting. Fiona learnt this lesson before me. Imagine when she grows up and gets a job and someone is going to have to be her boss; it's not going to happen is it? She's going to be their boss even though she works for them. We've never really had a matriarch in our family but I've got a nasty feeling at eleven years old she's plotting to take the title. One day she'll just announce at the dinner table, 'You all work for me now,' we'll disagree and she'll keep shouting it until we back down and say, 'OK we work for you now, just turn it down.'

Maybe when she's older and doing whatever high-powered job she does she'll have a business card, and after her name there will be an asterisk and then at the bottom of the card in small letters it will say, **Her family would like to apologise for creating a monster.*

It's not even like it was Ma or Da's fault; they did the same job with all of us. It's just she came out very clever and very opinionated. You can see Ma sometimes look at her after one of her episodes and realise that this is only going to get worse: I mean she's not even a teenager yet; this could be nothing compared to what's in store for us.

Anyway the point I'm making is I should have a bigger room but for what it's worth, it's not worth it.

Ma and Da are lucky they've got a lot less trouble with Sean; sure he's stupid and energetic like a puppy, but if you shout at him he'll do what's he's told. I wonder if Fiona took an extra brain quota so Sean was left with less.

Seriously the puppy thing is no joke. Ma sometimes says to us to take Sean on the green and give him a run out; if he doesn't get one he goes nuts in the house.

If his tongue was longer I'm sure it would hang out the side of his mouth.

When the station is on you have to tell him to calm down or feck off, as you can hear him bounding up the stairs. He's got this weird way of climbing the stairs where he uses his arms and legs, like a chimpanzee, and scrambles up.

We should just put some sort of generator on him; I'm sure we could power a lot of the house on his energy and stupidity.

Hey that's an idea, what about everybody in the world has a generator so that when they walk and run they power up a battery that they could plug in later. Like in physics, energy always goes somewhere, right? So we eat food that gives us energy, and we walk and burn that off, but when we walk and burn that off if we turned it back into energy we could harness that. That's a top idea, that one is getting written down.

I sometimes wonder if we're a normal family; like no one tells you if you are normal. Like clearly Davey's family are not normal, but then our family are we normal, normal-ish? I mean if you were normal wouldn't that be weird and make you abnormal?

I don't want to be normal, but then I don't want to be that far away from normal that I'm a freak; we're not freaks or anything. I think we're smart, I think we're a smartish family; that causes its problems but I think in general, like Da's obviously smart, Ma's smart, and she's got soul. Ma's definitely got soul, you can see it in her. I've never told her but she's cool. I've only just realised she's cool, like not 'cool' cool, like not trying to be cool: she's just got this steel in her, like you don't mess with her, you know she's got something in reserve that she could unleash. Da's scared of her, he loves her but you can see part of him knows to keep the right side of her, knows not to push it with her, she's got the power. He works for her.

So I'm walking back home from school. I'm even crap at walking, I just haven't got it down right, it's not something I do well. There are a number of things that I don't do well that I want to do better and I think I will one day but this I don't think I will ever get right.

It's not like I'm disabled and can't walk properly. I mean I can walk, it's just not very cool my walk; it's a scuttle, and the more I worry about it the worse my walk gets.

Basically I walk like the number 7 moving across the screen, hands in pockets, shoulders turned in and head down.

There's two reasons I'm a rubbish walker: one is I'm a bit lanky, so I suppose I stoop to compensate for this. I don't think you really get any good walkers that are tall; it's probably the distance between the brain and the feet. And that's my other problem: I don't think clever people can walk well. I'm reasonably clever, for this town anyway, and reasonably tall, therefore my walk is always going to be bad. If I were short and stupid my walk would be great. Stupid people can walk well, they don't worry about their walk. Why would they, they're stupid, so they just happily get on with it and let it happen, and that's the secret of a good walk, not to think about it; and because I know this secret, I am always going to be cursed by thinking about it and be crap at it.

The other thing about my stoop is the bloody wind; everyone in Clifden has to stoop a bit and pull their shoulders in because there is always a bloody wind in Clifden coming off the Atlantic. It travels a thousand miles with the express intent of making me cold. You know that fable about the sun and the wind trying to get that guy's coat off his back in the desert: honestly in this town you wouldn't even need the sun. If it would just stop blowing for one day, I tell you this town would have a carnival and all coats would be burnt in celebration.

What can I tell you about my hometown? It's got a population of about 2,000, it's on the upper west coast of Ireland but we're not quite north-west; there's another chunk before that.

I don't know what you'd most associate with our place. We're green, grey and green. In the summer we're green and blue, the rest of the year we are green and grey but we are always green, well once you get outside the town centre anyway.

In Iceland they have fifty words for snow: we should have two hundred for green, but we don't; we have one and we make it do for all the green of the countryside.

Connemara is God's own country: I know this as I am told it most days. 'It's a beautiful day, ah it's God's own country, so it is.' I wonder if he's got a holiday home here, as I've never seen him about.

Lots of people have holiday homes here; it's the joys of the Celtic bloody tiger. The Celtic tiger means we're all better off now, and when I say 'we' I mainly mean a bunch of people in Dublin and they've bought somewhere to go in the summer and made it bloody impossible for anyone else to buy anywhere except around the town centre which they don't want to buy near, as (*a*) it's not as pretty; and (*b*) there are people who actually live there day to day and they might just get called a few names on their way to the shop for pricing everyone else out of the nice spots.

But there's no doubt it's a beautiful area and I suppose you can't argue with people's desire to want to live here. I've grown up here all my life so I've kind of become immune to its beauty. I know it's pretty but I can't always see it; I'm just so used to it. When I go to Dublin which tends to happen about once a year I always think the place is just beautiful: the buildings, the people, the hustle; there's so much going on and that's what is beautiful, that's what fascinates me but then that's because I don't get to see it much. Imagine just imagine going to New York: it'd be like a nature geek going to the Amazon; I'd just get paralysed by the amount of stuff there.

Like if you live in Paris you are going to get bored of seeing that Eiffel Tower every day aren't you. Like, I know the hills are beautiful and all that but you just kind of get numb to them. I wonder once I'm in London if I'll appreciate them more. I wonder how I'll cope with so many people: what if it's too much for me? It won't be; I think I'll bloody love it. I can't wait to go on the Tube; it's going to be mad. All these miserable bastard commuters and me there just grinning, thinking, you don't know how lucky you are.

We're a pretty remote place and out of season you can really feel it. Galway is about sixty minutes away by car down the N59; by bus it's over an hour and a half, sometimes two. I usually go there about once a month either just to hang out or to buy stuff. Sometimes we'll do a whole family trip there but I'll drop them as soon as I get there and go to some record shops. If I don't go with the family then I'll go with Davey. I've only been for a night out there twice, it's such a pain in the arse to get back from so unless we've got someone who is prepared to drive us it's just not worth it. The last bus from Galway to Clifden is at 6.30 p.m. getting back just after 8 p.m.

The real bollix about Clifden being where it is, is that I never get to see any decent bands; they never come to us. It's rare they even go to Galway, especially if they are international. For example I've never seen a hip hop act. I bloody love hip hop; I've got to have about 300 hip hop tracks; I probably know more about hip hop than anyone in Clifden, which isn't hard; but I've never seen a hip hop act. I'm probably the only person in this town that has heard of Grime (though I still think it's shite). When I go to London I'm definitely going to see hip hop acts, I don't care if I am a pasty white bugger, I'm still going.

The only live music you are going to see in Clifden is folk acts, some of which are all right but you can't help but feel sometimes they're just doing it to milk the tourists, who have this idea in their head that they want to drink Guinness in a pub whilst some guy bangs away on a Bodhrán, while another guy either plays a fiddle or strums a guitar.

There are two indie bands in Clifden; I am friends with both of them. They are both shite, though I haven't told them this. One is Aviator, which is Patrick Cleen's lot;

they play your kind of generic indie, not very good, trying to be anthemic but just not getting close. I must've seen them over twenty times; every time I see them I have to say something positive to Patrick and it's getting harder and harder. He thinks when he is up there that any girl in the bar will see him and want him. Standing in front of a mic, on a guitar, makes girls want you if you're Jack White but then that's cos you're bloody Jack White; it doesn't work if you are Patrick Cleen as you're not Jack White, you're unfortunately Patrick Cleen and you've got a voice that sounds like a wolf being dragged behind a car.

The other band are called 2K as the only two people in the band are called Kyle and Karl (and even though the year 2000 was six years ago). I can't believe I am even talking about them as it means it will be recorded that they exist and in some distant part of the universe it will always be on record that they happened. Sweet Jesus they are awful, yet I've still seen them at least ten times.

You know how like bars in America have free salted snacks on the bar to make you drink more; bars in Clifden that put on either of these two acts use them as a way to get people to drink more, if only to make it bearable. If they locked the doors on the venue they would make a fortune as people raced to poison themselves with alcohol. The only cost would be having to pay every morning to get the windows redone after people had hurled themselves out of them as a means of escape.

I have to leave this place. I'm sure heaven is a nice place

but sooner or later you are going to want to go somewhere else even if it is just for a change of scenery.

So the other big influence on the town I haven't even mentioned is the sea; it's bloody cold. Only eejits and tourists go in it. And fishermen: they are not eejits, they are just lunatics; there's no way on God's earth I would even do a shift on one of those boats. They earn every penny they get.

I worry Davey will get a job on the boats; it's just the sort of profession that attracts head-the-balls like Davey.

The Maytals are thought to be the first act to use the term Reggae in their 1972 song 'Do the Reggay' (it's spelt Reggay as it was before people settled on it being spelt Reggae).

8

TUESDAY 16TH MAY

So my relationship with Doh is different than with the others in our sort of group. We're as clever as each other and in all honesty I reckon he'd be cleverer if he actually bothered to try. But there's also just a little bit of rivalry, but then I couldn't really say it was a rivalry because, as with everything, I'm sure he doesn't really care.

But the gang if anything is me and Doh – the clever ones, Danny the quiet one, Davey the random. We're not exactly the fucking A-Team; there's no leader, but that's who we are. But me and Doh have got the same role. Not that we are competing for air, but like we're probably the most similar in the group.

So this afternoon we are all in my room doing the radio station. Doh and Danny rarely come over to have anything to do with the station. This is probably because of Doh's distinct lack of interest. He's never shown any curiosity about the station other than to tell me which track was

'Wack'; he affects this ironic US hip hop gangsta language sometimes, so for him to show an interest should have worried me.

At school he was like, 'Hey can we come back to see the station, y'know, see the set-up,' and I bloody ought to have known better than to trust him to show keenness about anything. He probably had his little stunt planned from before and that's the evil bit.

You see with Doh, I like him, he's funny, we're friends, though not as close as me and Davey. He vaguely fascinates me in that he's clever, sarcastic and phenomenally cold, but I don't on any level trust him. I don't know why; maybe it is that same coldness: the lack of emotion means there's not as much to latch onto. I mean don't get me wrong, we are friends; we hang out a lot as he's good company, though mainly in a four, not as much just me and him. But he's cocksure and cold and I'm sometimes a little jealous of that: he doesn't care much about anything and I seem to care too much about everything.

So anyway they are round in my bedroom and I'm doing the 4 to 6 p.m. shift. The tracks are going through and I'm doing the odd bit of chat. Doh is trying to get me to put on a track by Goldie Lookin Chain called 'Your Mother's Got a Penis'. He thinks it will be funny and freak out some people. And it would be funny, but I have an audience to think about, and I have a responsibility to them, and what if some twelve-year-old girl hears it and says something to her parents. And that's Doh, he does something he thinks is funny and he doesn't care about the consequences.

And that's totally what he did this afternoon, the arsehole.

The radio station is playing 'Star Guitar' by the Chemical Brothers, and I start telling the others about the mad video that goes with it and end up getting it up on the screen for them to watch. I turn the station down a little and let a few tracks play into each other and they watch the song. So while they are watching it I pop out to the bog. There is a radio in there and I turn it on to hear what the signal is and listen to the end of the song playing when it's cut short and Doh comes on the mic in this muffled voice.

'This is an appeal on behalf of a young man named Lex Donal. In three months' time our Lex, your radio host, is leaving the motherland for the big smoke of London. But he goes there not complete, not a real man; he goes there with no swagger in his stride, people: he goes there a virgin.

'In the time he has left in our fair town would some fair girl please put this poor fella out of his misery. He's a lovely lad and he's clean; make his summer and turn him into a man. Thank you for listening.

'"Pity rides" will be gladly welcomed.

'This has been a broadcast on behalf of the People's Movement for Lex's Virginity, the PMLV. Thanks for listening.'

I'm having a slash when I hear this and I can't stop so I rush and try to finish and get out and some runs down my leg. Then I'm banging like startled horse on my bedroom door, and the fuckers have got a chair wedged against the handle. When one of them finally moves it I get in the room to find them all in hysterics.

I'm so bloody angry: it's such an out-of-order thing to do. At first I'm just stood there shouting 'WHAT THE FUCK DID YOU DO THAT FOR?' over and over again. I mean I'm genuinely upset and it doesn't help that they think it's the best thing since donkey dicks.

I think about which one to hit first and end up hitting none of them, though I do get Doh in a headlock as he's obviously the ringleader, but it is made pretty futile as he won't stop laughing and I have to let him go.

I call him a fucking langer and turn the computer off; the station signal gets cut off for the rest of the day. Not that it's going to do me much good now.

He's such a cockwipe sometimes.

I tell them to fuck off out my house, and they happily skip out patting each other on the back and high-fiving.

I mean that is so, so out of order. I would never do something that humiliating to them.

And Davey is the one I am most annoyed at. He didn't do anything to stop it; he just let it happen. Doh had to have suggested it before he did it and Davey has just gone along with it.

Me and Davey are supposed to be proper mates. Yeah maybe there was peer pressure, but surely Davey could have stood up to that. Now I'm never going to hear the end of it.

Also Doh doesn't know for sure I'm a virgin. Only Davey knows for sure as he's the only one I've ever talked about it with and so he must've told him which is another betrayal.

*

The phone starts beeping and all sorts of texts start coming in. I'm totally morto'd.

I have nine messages. These include:

> VIRGIN!!!
> HA HA HA AH HA
> I'll do you and so will my friend. Love LP
> Ha ha loser
> *Raises fist to PMLV*
> Your [sic] cute
> Oh Dear Lexxy boy

And finally:

> Wanker! (To be fair, I usually have one or two a day that just say 'Wanker', 'Gaylord' or 'Shitehead' so this could just be coincidental.)

My face is red and I'm raging. Most people know who I am because of the radio station; so now they all know I'm a virgin, and when I meet people they are going to smile at me half with amusement and half with pity. Michelle would have heard it and now definitely won't have anything to do with me: girls only want to ride a bloke if he knows what he's doing. Up until this moment of my life any humiliation I've ever felt has always been on a minor level; not that it felt minor at the time, but it was always localised, where only anyone in the immediate vicinity could share in my embarrassment. Now I have suffered public humiliation and it makes me feel sick; I think my glands have started running.

The only saving grace was I don't think Ma and Da were listening today and Sean and Fiona haven't said anything so far; if they do I may have to kill them. I didn't say a word over dinner.

I'm going to be like a leper in the town now; everyone is going to stop and point and say, there goes the virgin. Christ even Mrs O'Dowd is going to look down at me: at least she's had a shag in her lifetime, which is better than I'm doing.

There's got to be some way to get him back. I start plotting but can't seem to get past the idea of stabbing him, with a twelve-foot metal lance.

What it lacks in wit it makes up for in directness and honesty.

I plan to search eBay for lances; I wonder if I will need a horse to stick it in him or maybe a tank.

I should add to this that two days later I'm walking into town and on the small brick wall by the bus stop on the way into town is PMLV in white foot-high paint. It's not the last I'll see this summer. I text Doh, who for the rest of this story might well be called Shitehead, with: 'Graffiti?'

The one I get back from him just says: 'Art?'

To which I reply: 'Dead Meat.'

The cocky bastard only comes back to that too with: 'Modern Art?'

I know it's him who did it.

One of their best songs, and possibly their most famous, is called '54–46 Was My Number'. It's an absolute classic. It was originally recorded as '54–46 That's My Number' before being re-recorded. It's about the eighteen months in 1966–67 when Toots was sent to prison on a marijuana possession charge. His prison number was 54–46.

9

I could do worse for a role model than my mother and father. They're all right when you think about them. I know people who got a lot worse in the parent department. I mean they're not cool or anything but then who really wants cool parents? You're only going to rebel against them anyway, so if I had cool parents it would be even worse for me, and besides I want parents who are going to be my parents, not these tragics who won't grow up and just want to be the kid's friend.

They're not bad though. Da works for himself as an accountant; he does the accounts for lots of the businesses in town, so he seems to know everyone who owns a business. I don't think he minds it; he likes meeting and chatting to people. I think the chore bit of it is just something he deals with. He's lived in Clifden all his life; his parents, who are both gone now, they lived about a mile from us.

I asked him why once, about sticking in the same town all his life. He said he never really wanted to go anywhere else; that it was plenty grand here. That kind of limited thinking can actually be a good thing; it leads to contentment and happiness. If you settle for the really uncomplicated and the unstretched dream then you are likely to fulfil it, and as long as you don't question it, you are going to be satisfied. It frustrates me but I admire it at the same time; there isn't a word for that, is there? Something that you admire but frustrates you: I should come up with a word for that. I could ask Mr Hickey or I could set it as a competition on the radio. It's a bit philosophical for the shop workers I think; another one for the notepad.

Look at Sean and Fiona. Sean's dream is to find a crisp as big as his hand and get it all in his mouth without it cracking, and God bless that boy because one day he's going to achieve that dream and that is going to be a happy and fulfilled young man. Fiona on the other hand wants to be a lawyer and a dancer and a fashion designer and a pop star, this is not a lawyer *or* a dancer *or* a fashion designer *or* a pop star: she wants to do all four at once. This is going to lead to disappointment further down the line; life is going to be full of disappointments for that girl.

I couldn't do it Da's way; I've got to get away. Not that I don't love this town, it's just that I've done everything that there is to do here twenty times now. Apart from that I want to go to London: I want to go to the Astoria, and Rough Trade Records and the 100 Club, and hang out in Shoreditch with music journalists, writers and things and drink in Camden with new bands. There's so much I want to do over there; it's going to be unreal.

I've been reading loads about it: I mean it's massive, and

there's like these killer bands on every night. I'm going to be broke by the end of the first week. I'm scared and excited: is there a word for that too? Exshite-ed maybe? Not worth writing down, that one.

I'm toying with the idea of reinventing myself over there, cos like I don't want them to think of me as some kind of naive culchie. People in Ireland already think we are rural and backward; in London they're going to think – I dunno what they'll think. I wonder if the accent will work a charm. I'm just not that sort of fella though; I'm not a charmer, I don't do the charm thing. Christ I'm only seventeen; I'm a bit young to have charm. You're not going to get charm until you're in your twenties at least.

Going to have to get better at dancing too. Like at the Electric Picnic, I was drunk in one of the tents and I'm just pure going for it, and people are just looking at me like I'm a fruit. I was just gonna go for it, but y'know it was mega and the music was just going through me and that was it. I'm not one of these posey guys y'know, I'm down the front, a sweaty gangly thing, and I'm going to go for it. It's not cool but I don't give a shit, and those D4 Dubliners they can go fuck themselves cos I was having a right time of it I was.

But it did annoy me afterwards, like don't just laugh at someone, it ruins the vibe man. I'm just expressing myself, why start laughing and pointing? They were these snobby sunglasses-inside lot though, thought they were the bollocks; well I'd rather be a sweaty dancer than a snobby posey shitestain.

So anyway my Da, his dreams have always been quite limited in my opinion. I'd still say he is a clever man, but not just clever: he's wise too, and I think there's a difference between the two. Like you can be clever and know a lot of facts or you can be wise and know what to do with them.

Maybe Da's desire to lead a quieter life was the wise decision; maybe me going to London will lead me to learning more but getting less.

Da once said that perspective dictates life. Understand perspective and you'll understand life.

Da says a lot; it's a rare thing that actually sticks with me. It's funny cos I think he's imparting his finest wisdom and these pieces are the building blocks for the making of me, but the blocks don't always stay stuck.

He's a very calming influence on my life though; he's just a calm man. I hope one day I will be as calm as him. I wonder if his calmness has come with age. I find myself getting less and less calm as I'm getting older; I just keep finding more things to worry about.

Anyway the thing he said that stuck was: of the people at his school who aren't still his friends he can only really remember one fact about each of them. The entire ten years he may have been at school with them will be boiled down into one incident. Sometimes those incidents define their character; sometimes they don't. Like the girl in his class whose hair caught fire on a Bunsen burner: it burnt it all up and she had to have it all shaved off and start again.

She may go on to become anything but will always be known as the girl whose hair caught fire.

Matthew will always be the guy who pissed himself in a physics lesson.

If I fuck up this festival I will be the guy who fucked up the festival, unless I manage to achieve something even more tragic than that.

Is it shallow to think I might not be friends with these people in the future? I'm just being realistic. When I go to London things are going to change. I'll still be friends with Davey.

Ma is Ma, and she's lovely. She works part-time at the bakery, so she gets top-quality bread for us every day. She met Da when he ventured out to Galway for an evening; she's a Galway girl. She's quite a bit smaller than me but she's never lost that loving air of a violence that cares; that if I step out of line I'm going to get a clout so hard my eardrums will ring for a week.

And as for the siblings, Sean's a wee fecker and Fiona is a gobshite; I think I might have implied that with some of the earlier stuff. I'll fill you in about them later on, if I haven't killed the pair of them by then.

Other big songs of theirs include 'Pomps & Pride', 'Pressure Drop', 'Do the Reggay', 'Monkey Man', 'Sweet and Dandy', 'Funky Kingston', 'Reggae Got Soul', 'Time Tough', 'Broadway Jungle' and of course 'Take Me Home Country Roads'. They are all deadly.

10

MA

Lex is my big soldier. It's so strange how big he is now, to think he was so wee, and he's so bright now too. He's much cleverer than me; he could be cleverer than his father soon, if he's not already. His father tries to keep one step ahead of him by reading the *Indo* before Lex gets down in the morning so he's more informed, but he won't be able to do that for long. If Lex goes off to London to college then when he comes back I think he will be ahead of him.

The daft pair spar at the moment to see which one knows more. His dad wins at Trivial Pursuit if they play, but then we've had that set so long Michael has seen all the questions ten times over. I may buy a new set then see how his dad gets on, or better still just slip in a new set of questions without him knowing.

Lex hasn't been playing him much recently what with his exams and this silly concert; I wish he'd forget about the concert until his exams are over. The exams take so much out of him both physically and emotionally; he has to do so many of them. He's been doing them for years now and there's always another set ahead of him. I'm hoping this is the last big lot before college; these are the ones that matter the most. His school are impressed with how he's doing; they always said he could do a bit better and apply himself more but I think that he works hard enough at his subjects.

I don't want him to go to London, but I can't stop him. It's too far away and it's too big; I don't know how he'll cope with a place that big. It scares the life out of me, places that big: Dublin is bad enough. We went to New York once and I tell you that place just gave me a headache something chronic. Millions of people, like rats they were, scurrying around everywhere, spitting on the streets and all, it was disgusting.

I wanted him to go to Dublin, as it's not too far and we could pop down if he was in trouble, but he always wanted to go to London ever since that music boy Andrew Farn at school went over there and came back and filled his head with ideas.

We can always fly over there; it only takes an hour from Galway airport, and we could go over and see a show or something, maybe make a weekend of it.

It's going to cost money though and he's going to end up seriously in debt. I know he's got some saved up from his website stuff, if he doesn't spend it all on this concert. He doesn't know we've got a bit saved up as an emergency for him. We started putting a bit aside each month from when he was twelve and it became clear he was really bright and would probably need to go to college. He's the first Donal I know of that's gone to college. My sister's boy Euan went last year but none have gone on Michael's side of the family.

We are going to have to start a saving pot soon for Fiona, as she seems a smart one as well. Poor Sean, bless, I don't think there's too much danger of him troubling a university campus but you never know, he could surprise us all, and besides they do courses for everything nowadays so it's only a matter of time before they do one in computer games.

I don't want Lex to get his heart broken by this girl he likes, but then you need to let them don't you; he needs to get his heart broken once or they will walk all over you. I know he'll be grand in the long run but I don't want to see him get hurt.

He just needs a nice girl. I'm sure there are plenty that would take him but he has to go for Miss Unattainable to make himself all miserable.

It's not even like it's hard to get a girl these days. It was a lot different in my day, very different; now girls will drop their breeches if you just look at them. I'm glad if he's going to do that sort of thing that he's going to do that in London: I don't want him getting himself a reputation around here. We are a decent family, a known family and I don't want them to think my Lexxy is a womaniser but he needs a bit of experience to make him more of a man.

I'm sure I'm worried about nothing; he's a smart lad, but

he's a teenage boy and there's a limit on how clever they can get. Lex is a clever boy but emotionally I sometimes think he can be a bit immature. I hope he ends up getting the right balance.

It's so strange to think of him as nearly a man now. He's shot up so much in the last two years; he's even got a little bit of stubble and some hair on his chest and some lean muscles on him. Honestly there's not an ounce of fat but he never does any exercise. He was always one of the smaller boys at school; it wasn't until puberty that he really caught up with the others. I know he was really worried about that too: he's never liked sport at the best of times but when you are up against boys much bigger than you it can't be much fun. I also know he used to skip his PE classes sometimes. He never found out that we knew but the teacher would tell us on parents' evening, or mention the excuse notes he had written. I couldn't tell him off though and to be honest I think the teacher actually felt sorry for him too. You can't force the boy to do it if he doesn't want to: what's the point; Lex was never destined for sport, he's a thinker. You don't force the thickies to take the same maths tests as the bright ones but everyone has to do sport together.

I know that us mothers are just preparing them and getting them ready to be set free but part of me really wants to keep him home and locked up for me. I've started to cry about it now that it's so close. I can be in the kitchen and sometimes I'll just start crying. Michael says it could be 'the change', the unsympathetic eejit, but it breaks my heart to think I won't see him for three whole months at a time.

I can't do anything to help him once he's across the water. Here I can make things better for him if they go wrong, and they will go wrong and I've just got to stay here and let it happen. Over there I'm just going to be a voice on the phone; not that he'll ring me, boys never phone home unless they need more money.

And once he's gone out into the world he won't come back the same. The world will change him, London will change him and he won't be my Lex any more. Michael won't even talk to me about it, he just says to stop being a woman about it: well, I am a woman and I'll be how I want about it.

He's my little treasure.

11

SATURDAY 20TH MAY

Wake up still drunk. I have twenty seconds of peace before the fear strikes me. I've had the fear before, the morning after and not knowing what I did and the fear that it is as bad as my worst imagination would have me believe. I think this time it's worse.

I get occasional blackouts when I drink too much: I simply can't remember what has happened to me the night before. I think this is a protection mechanism. I think the brain is just deleting the tapes of my drunken behaviour. I think my mind is saying, when you are drunk you act like such a dick that I don't want you to have to see this. You'd think so much less of yourself if you did.

Anyway the fear is here, and it's a double fear; it's bad this time. I'm still in my clothes for one; I'm on my bed, not in it. There are two buttons missing on my shirt and the collar is torn away from the neck a bit.

Think, Lex.

I don't feel bruised at all. My knuckles don't look like I've been fighting; I couldn't have been that bad. My head doesn't hurt but I know it will in an hour or so. I roll off the bed and onto the floor. I think I'll just stay here a while before I get myself up. Floors are always good places in times of crisis.

I drift back to sleep even though I'm on the floor and am woken by Ma calling from downstairs: Davey is at the door. She shouts, 'David is here!' She always calls him David; not even his own mother calls him David. I think she thinks giving him his respectable fully pronounced name will make him be more respectable and better behaved and not get me into trouble. My response is too slow and she sends him straight up to my room.

He leaps into the room and is bouncing around with noisy energy. I try to calm him down.

'What a night!' he says. 'What a night!' again, and then: 'You nearly got your arse kicked.'

'Did I?' I reply, trying to stop him moving.

'Did you? My God did you? If Dansey didn't know who you were before, he sure as shite does now, holy mother of God!'

My headache has arrived. Davey brought it with him. I don't want to know what happened but I regret that it's my destiny to find out.

I'm sat on the side of my bed now with my face in my hands. I still reek of last night. I don't know how he's so up about it all. He's even shaved this morning. He must have shaved with the excitement of it all. He shaves about once a week, and he's shaved just to come over and tell me what a mess I was last night.

'Say . . .,' I start, '. . . if one were not quite able to piece together all the incidents of last night; say if that were to be the case, would you be able to maybe fill in the major details and events of the evening just for, you know, recollection purposes?'

'What, you mean you can't remember? Oh man, it was legend, you were roasting.'

His face is filled with glee: he's desperate to tell me what happened, and his mouth is ready to burst with the information. I nod for him to proceed.

And he begins, but moving round the room all the while. 'So I got to the pub at 9 p.m. after the dinner service as I was doing a double and you were drunk when I got there; you were there with Danny and Doh. And they were like just chatting to each other and you were with them at the table but you weren't if you see what I'm saying. You were sat with us but you were only with us half the time; the rest of the time you were just staring. I mean you were definitely pissed at 9 p.m. You know how you get all mopey and shite when you go all quiet: I think it's your brains. I may be thick but I know one thing; too many brains doesn't make for happy. Anyway we were trying to include you in the chat and you'd be fine for ten minutes or so then you'd just stop and go back into your mope.' He continues: 'Yeah an' then so after ten, Liam Dansey and two of his buds come in.'

I feel sick in my stomach now, I know the story of me

is going to collide with the story of Liam and I know I'm not going to be pleased with the outcome.

'So he's come in and he's at the bar, only you don't notice cos you've got your back to the main bar and you're facing us. About 10.30 p.m. it's your round but you'd been mumbling stuff about Michelle, so I head off to get the round after persuading you you'd just got one, so that you wouldn't bump into him. Anyway I think I'm clever and so until I bring the drinks back and you're sat in my seat now, facing the bar. And . . .'

I interrupt. 'Wait – shouldn't you be at the hotel right now?'

'Day off. So anyway you're facing the room and the next thing you see Liam and you start staring at him. And I've taken your seat and I'm trying to stick my head in the way so you have to look at me but you're staring round me. Doh's bird, oh yeah I forgot Doh's bird Stella, so she'd joined us about ten: she starts trying to get you to engage with her and distract you from Liam but all you kept doing was like mumbling, and one of your eyes was going lazy. Do you know your eyes go all over the gaff when you're really polluted? I've never seen you do that before, probably because when you're that wasted, so am I. So Stella, she's trying to distract you; I'm trying to stop you from staring at him, and in general it was a bit of a baby-sit, that's until you discover the word "Ballbag". You were mumbling something for a while and it gradually got more and more clear.

'So you says it again a bit louder and the table next to

us, which was these fifty-year-old tourists, two couples, they hear you and start looking over all offended. Stella apologises, then you say it again, but you're not saying it at anyone, like you're just saying it, spraying it; I mean you were just twisted and rambling. Then you do it again and it's louder, not quite a shout but a firm "Ballbag!" and you're looking for Liam.

'I turn around to see if he's heard you but luckily he's not there, he's gone. His buds are still there though. Then you shout "BALLBAG!" loud, and the whole place looks round. And we're trying to get you to stop it: you're not angry or nothing, you're just saying this thing. Danny and Doh are pissing themselves and Stella is trying to put her hand over your gob. But you pull it down and shout "BALLBAG!" again. And everyone turns round to look at you again. You decide to look back at them and smile: but it was this right menacing smile, you know like that fat guy you do that impression of in *Full Metal Jacket*. Michael looks over to us from the bar as if to say "calm him down".

'Then it happens. Liam has just been at the toilets; he comes back round the bar and you spot him. You stand up at the table and you bloody point at him and you shout "BALLBAG!!!"

'Doh's under the table in convulsions, Stella is trying to get you to sit down, then you go into machine gun mode: "BALLBAG! BALLBAG! BALLBAG! BALLBAG! BALLBAG! BALLBAG! BALLBAG!" All the time you're pointing at Liam. It was unreal. I mean it was hilarious, if it wasn't going to get us all killed.

'Everyone's staring at you now. Michael comes out from behind the bar and tells us all we've got to go. He grabs you and forces you out, only you are trying to explain that he shouldn't be throwing you out because you are not the ballbag.

'We get outside right and you can hardly stand, and worse, you're actually disgusted that we've been thrown out at all and you're wanting to get back in. Eventually we calm you down and start walking back home but as we get round the corner Liam and his posse are standing there waiting for you; they'd come out the other side of the pub.

'And they are fuming. I thought they were going to tear into all of us. I think they are his mates from the footy team; they looked like they'd snap you in half, you know what I mean?

'And faced with the beating of your life you did the cleverest thing I've ever seen you do: you started to laugh at him, like uncontrollably laughing at him and pointing. Then you start rolling on the floor, like absolutely wetting yourself and every now and then you stop the rolling then point at him again then start creasing up again. I mean you should be sectioned man, you are not well. If I wasn't so scared too I'd've been laughing with you, but I was just waiting for him to start laying into us.

'But it was genius man, cos what can he do, he can't start wading into a guy who is already on the floor?

'Only problem is cos he can't have a go at you he now starts coming towards me, but this is when we totally fuck with his head.'

Davey starts laughing now.

'Please tell me this story doesn't get worse,' I say.

'Oh no, it just gets better. I pulled the Crane . . .'

I shake my head. 'Please no,' I say.

'No I did, totally *Karate Kid*: one-legged Crane motherfucker.'

Davey and I had watched the Crane clip from *Karate Kid* on YouTube over and over again. Davey had talked before about having a death move; he likes that American wrestling rubbish and they have each got their personal death move. He wanted one of his own.

'Go on . . .' I say, stunned by how last night could get stupider.

'Well then they just started laughing at me. Doh and Stella were laughing at me too; you were still on the floor laughing at Liam.

'But the thing is it worked, the Crane worked, they backed off. I think they were laughing through nervous fear at the vengeance I could wreak. They feared the Crane.'

I sit on the edge of my bed still looking at the floor and for the first time smile.

'Do you think he's going to come after me?' I ask.

'Not likely, but if you tell him you want to ride his missus I'm sure he won't leave you on the floor next time. I swear to God, Lex, it was awesome.'

'Awesome for you maybe; thank Christ I'm getting out this town soon. Do you think I should apologise?'

'Nah, technically he is a ballbag so you've nothing to apologise for. Right then,' he says, 'it's my day off. I'm going into Galway; my Ma's taking me in so got to get there sharpish. Aren't you supposed to be on the radio now?'

'Oh shit!' I start trying to find some clean clothes and turn on the PC.

'Enjoy the hangover, Padre. Pint when I get back?'

'No way.'

I hate Coldplay too. I think it is mainly because they are dad-rock-indie-anthem-by-number sub-sub-Radiohead-derivative-generic crap. And Bono is a twat.

12

TUESDAY 23RD MAY

Tuesday night again, salsa again, sandwich-buying again. Fiona asks for only organic vegetables in her sandwich this time. I'm walking home from the supermarket carrying three baguettes in my arms. Michelle was looking gorgeous while making the sandwiches as usual; I wonder if she looks forward to Tuesday at half six as much as I do. She probably doesn't notice I've been in thirty-two Tuesdays in a row between 6.30 p.m. and 7 p.m. Even the weeks Ma and Da didn't do salsa I still came in as I didn't want to break the chain. I thought it might be bad luck: not that it has brought me too much good luck with her so far.

The weather is glorious this early summer's evening. The sun is getting cool as it goes off towards America, the clouds are broken and scattered, and amazingly it's not raining or looking like it is just about to start raining.

I nip between the parked cars and march back home. I'm starving and want to get in one final hour's revision before I stop for the day. I'm trying to do it in block hours, and if I manage six hours it has been a good day; less than six it's bad. I did five yesterday so am going to try to do seven today, keep the average up. Hopefully the hours will pay off.

I'm thinking whether I should spend more time on my better subjects to get higher marks, or if it would be better spent on the areas I'm weaker giving me a higher average, and that's when I see Patrick O'Shea and his small posse of brain donors. Patrick O'Shea was in my year at school until he dropped out. He would only come sporadically and then just stopped coming at all. The teachers didn't mind, as when he came in he would only spend the time disrupting everyone. There was a rumour he only stopped coming in as he was so thick he had forgotten the way.

He was pretty hard in our year; I wonder why God seems to give a lot of the thick ones muscles? I wonder if it's part of his master plan as there are a lot of big heavy things to be lifted in this world, like fridges, and you don't need too many brains to lift stuff, so why overburden a fella with brains and muscles.

But he was rock, second hardest in our year. Only person harder was Michael Playte; he was just a massive gentle giant, didn't want to hurt anyone unless he absolutely had to. Forced into playing GAA because of his size when he didn't want to, he was almost like a giant baby, and seemed embarrassed by his strength. He was the one person O'Shea couldn't mess with.

But O'Shea was hard in his own right and pig-thick stupid. His 'crew' consisted of his younger brother and two of his younger brother's mates. If I have a kid I'm going to tell him always be wary of guys at seventeen/eighteen who hang around with younger lads and don't hang about with any lads their own age: this is probably because by sixteen most of the people their own age have concluded that they are a dick.

These youngsters he knocks round with all look up to him, and cackle at his jokes like demented gremlins.

Patrick O'Shea is an anchor on the human race, slowing us down, dragging us backwards. Darwin doesn't work fast enough sometimes. I suppose as a species leaps forward, once in a while there's a regression.

So as I'm walking past I see them sitting on a low wall, three of them, one of the youngsters just kicking the wall gently with the toe of his runners.

'Les, ya wankstain,' calls out O'Shea as I approach, and his bridesmaids faithfully howl with appreciation. O'Shea calls me Les, not Lex: it's short for Lesbian and sounds similar to Lex which is my name, so I hope you can appreciate what the genius has done there. Other gems from him can include Lexbian, Lesbos, Lexbos, Donal Duck, Donal Fuck, Les Fuck-a-Duck; the list is seemingly endless. Strangely I've rarely heard him bestow the honour of so many nicknames on others, so I could be considered truly blessed.

I nod to him and mumble a 'howareya?' as I get close, so I can just continue on and not waste a moment more than I absolutely have to sharing time with this boil. 'Not so fast Lesley!' he says and holds out an arm to stop me.

I forgot Lesley is also a name he calls me: it's a girl's name sometimes. I am to him a girl, you see now, hilarious.

'Hey lads . . .' says O'Shea, addressing his little pack. 'Did you know Lexxy here is a virgin?' They roar with laughter, I sigh with resignation. 'Lexxy has never done it with a girl!' One of the little feckers starts hopping round and clapping; another starts chanting, 'Lexxy is a virgin, Lexxy is a virgin.' I'm not taking this shit from bloody thirteen-year-olds but there's nothing I can do: clip one of them and O'Shea will flatten me. He's just toying with me so his cubs have something to play with. I'm in a nature documentary and I'm the wounded baby zebra.

'Very good, Patrick,' I say, trying to sound as bored and uninterested as I can. The more you rise to it, the happier it will make him. It's so bloody embarrassing though, the whole town knows the weak point at which to jab you. Doh, I will hurt you so bad some day.

I smile a shite-eating smile and say, 'Glad you're a listener, Patrick.'

'I wouldn't listen to that wank,' comes the reply. 'I just heard they're starting a collection to get you a big fat whore before you feck off.'

I let out another sigh: I am the town charity case, the town joke, an embarrassment to my family and myself. I go to carry on home when one of the jumping wee shites knocks a baguette out of my hands. I reach out to swing at him with my free arm and catch the back of his head, at which point O'Shea pushes himself off the wall and delivers a straight hammer of a punch to my left arm. It fucking kills; the pain goes up and down my arm and I drop the other sandwiches as I let out a yelp.

O'Shea then stamps on the baguettes turning them into mush, whilst pointing and shouting, 'Don't you fucking ever touch my brother ya fuck.' The pain in my arm has now raced all over my body: I think I'm in shock. The others join in stamping on the baguettes and I walk off back to the supermarket feeling morto.

'You must be starving,' says Michelle after I order again. I smile without separating my lips: I think I'm going to cry; she doesn't ask any more. If she were twenty years older and not so attractive I would happily break into tears and wail until I got the hug I was after.

I mope to the till, then mope back home, this time on the other side of the road. O'Shea and the shitebags are still there; they hurl bits of veg at me from the remains of the last sandwiches. They hit the car I'm walking beside, and I continue home trying to ignore them.

God if there's any burning ambition in me, it is not to let that sack of crap do better than me in life. How can you explain to someone that thick the delight you will have in ten years' time when you come back to see them as a store detective.

Some people say at the end of the day that you are only racing against yourself and the goals and targets that you set yourself but I'm not, I'm racing against arseholes like him who I want to trounce, to make the shit they have given me worthwhile.

On the way back I fantasise about becoming a scientist

inventor who invents new types of weapons so that I could come home and test them out on O'Shea and the other cretins in our town. I wonder if inventors of modern war machines like tanks and missiles were originally motivated by bullies they wanted to obliterate with more and more powerful machines. The ultimate show of the brain being mightier than the moron, or how bullying led to the H-bomb.

I am aware Bono is not in Coldplay but he is still a twat. I think Chris Martin might be all right actually, because he also suspects he is a twat and thus takes the sting out of any thoughts I might have.

13

SEAN

Lex is quite cool. But Lex is also quite bad. He gets everything his way in our house.

If he doesn't get his way he shouts until Mum makes us do what he wants.

He sometimes tries to give me a dead arm but he's rubbish at it and can never do it right, not like Andy Taylor's brother Tommy: his dead arms kill. He's a bad bully, he locked us both in a cupboard for two hours and we couldn't get out, then he left the house and it wasn't until his mum came home and heard us that we got out. I told Lex so he would go and sort him out but he didn't do anything. He's as tall as Tommy but I don't think he could fight him. I don't think Lex wants to fight anyone; he's not very tough.

But at least Andy's brother will play ball with us sometimes. Lex never will; I don't think he can. I'm better at footy than Lex and he's eight years older than me; he's not very good with his arms and legs.

Lex is brainy though, he's a swot. Fiona is a swot too. Dad is brainy as well. I'm OK, Mum says I should concentrate more and stop getting into trouble but I don't mean to.

In our house everyone has to treat Lex special, because he's got exams, which is unfair. If anything upsets Lex he goes and tells Mum or Dad and they shout at us to stop. You can't do anything in our house at the moment: the computer is too loud, TV is too loud, walking on the stairs is too loud.

He won't even let us have a go on his computer. I've got a PlayStation2 which is deadly, but he's got some brilliant games on his computer but he won't let me play them.

Sometimes he'll play me at a racing game or Streetfighter and like he's never practised or nothing but he'll win after two goes and then you can't beat him. I'm the best for my age at Streetfighter, no one my age has beaten me ever.

14

I'm not a good exam-taker. I don't think I would ever want to be friends with someone who was a good exam-taker; it's not a quality I would find endearing in a human being. Anyway I hate it: the pressure, the nerves; if you are a sportsman in a cup final and nervous, at least once it starts you can run it off. I suppose in an exam you can write your nerves off, but it's not the same.

I mean, what's not to be nervous of: every time you sit down in these manky halls your life is getting decided. One bad exam could fuck the whole thing up. There is that much pressure in the room on all us hopeless retards that I wouldn't be surprised if one of us started weeping. Then the whole lot would start bawling and breaking down.

I sit down at the desk. Always the same routine: check it doesn't wobble too much; I take some card to adjust the desk. I check mine isn't too close to the person in front or behind or to the sides: I need my personal space to panic in. My pencil case is a resealable kitchen sandwich bag; we're supposed to have clear bags so we can't cheat, but so far everyone else has a normal pencil case. I have my passport and registration number to prove who I am. I fill out my number onto the sheets (no names), my desk position, the date, the exam code. I guess this is just to occupy you while waiting for the off. All the exams are three hours long; it's the physical limit for writing before a human hand will fall off.

You know, for the amount of shite you go through for these they should just give them to you: they should say at the end, 'Honestly, if you want it so much to go through with this then you can just have it.'

I'm surprised for what we get put through that more exam boards aren't burnt to the ground every May/June. Whoever did that would be held as a hero to students everywhere. Never mind Che Guevara posters: if there was one student who went around burning exam papers and exam boards setting us all free, they would be canonised by the National Union of Students.

These exams are fucking ridiculous anyway. All they test is who can memorise the most things possible, and who can interpret what the examiner is wanting. Like there's so much information on the Internet anyway that you don't need to memorise information: the information is out there; you just need to be able to access it.

The future is not going to be changed by who has got the most memory. The future is going to be changed by people who can think differently, but that is not what exams measure: they are just a linear measurement about memory. Apart from maths: maths is puzzle-solving; that one you use your brain and actually think in the exams to beat a problem, the rest you just download information you've memorised.

What if you were like really clever with a shit memory: exams are going to show you are rubbish, but you might be really clever. They should test us on our first day and about anything that will show you what we know and how smart we are already before the prepping.

It's not even like they reward original thinking. They know the answers they are looking for; the teachers know how to teach us to answer the questions in the way that will pick up the most marks, not the way that understands the subject best. I hope college is more about original thinking, like original economic thinking. I like debate and that, ideas battles, not just rote memorising.

I know from the last four exams onwards I will be dreaming of the total and utter genocide I am going to commit on my brain cells with the help of alcohol. My brain will be wiped clean of all facts within two hours of that final exam. I will be like an EtchASketch, shaken so there is no trace of what was there before. I will be a clean slate, a mind free from the tyranny of exams.

My brain cells will be like soldiers returning from war; they will be used up and spent and the government will no longer have any need for them and will discard them, no matter the huge sacrifice they have made on our behalf. Those facts and cells are a sorry reminder of a time we would rather forget, a stain on our history: it's best we never talk of them again; I cannot bear to even look at you.

Maybe I am being a bit melodramatic. Maybe this isn't the be-all and end-all, maybe I am being a bit over-the-top about my plight and this section will be a tiny footnote in the grand story of Lex Donal Worldwide Radio Star, but this is how it feels at the centre of Operation Please-let-me-pass-these-exams-and-get-out-of-the-slow-death-I-am-experiencing-in-this-town, and it feels like if I don't get this, all the other stuff that could happen isn't going to happen and I'm going to get stuck here.

15

DAVEY

Lex is my best mate. I'm not sure why he's my best mate but he is. He's way cleverer than me, but having said that he's shite at sport, so I guess we are equal overall.

Lex is over to London soon as his brain is so big Ireland cannot take it. It will be a pisser when he goes but it'll be all right I suppose.

I might go over and see him and get some English girls. They love our accent apparently which will do me; maybe I can bag one of the girls from his college or something.

Lex has got big plans and dreams. If they come off maybe he'll need a minder or somebody. Maybe he'll need a right-hand man on the radio. Failing that I could be his cook. If he got on telly, I could be like his cookery guy. I'm working at the Continental and I'm definitely getting better. Chef is a real gonad, he's an old alkie bollix and leathered after 9 p.m., but I'm picking up bits of knowledge off him when he's sober.

I'm cooking meats now, which is a decent move for me. I've been there eighteen months; I've done starters and done garde manager, which is like the fridge manager or cold foods section. It's feckin hot on the grill like but it's the best part of the kitchen, slinging the meat on and seeing it sizzle and all. Chef gives me loads of shit if I fuck up a piece of meat cos they're real expensive like, but when I get it right and get a 'perfect, Spaz' or do a whole service and don't fuck up once then I feel like the nuts. Even then though Chef can be a real arse but he never remembers the drunken rants so none of us listen to him from that point onwards. I'm sure he's going to drop dead soon anyway. He doesn't look good; he's always banging pills in his office. Dravo, who's Polish and the sous-chef, says we should bet on when he dies.

I get called 'Spaz' in the kitchen; it's cos I kept fucking up at the start and Chef kept calling us 'Spaz', then the others did. I only let them call me it as I was new but it stuck. Now I only let the older ones call me it. This new junior commis called me 'Spaz' and I pinned the little fucker up against the wall and bit his nose, and he soon stopped doing that.

It's a pisser Lex going but I'll be grand; I'll still see him and all. I should probably get myself a bird, give me something to do, or maybe hang about with Danny and Doh a bit more. There's no way I can be arsed taking on the radio station: Lex asked me but it's too much time and for not too much benefit from what I can see. Fair enough if you want to become a radio DJ like Lex does but I don't really want to do that as a job as I'm not really that much of a twat, which seems to be the starting point for most of the guys on the radio. I suppose Lex has got a head start in that case.

He's a good lad an' all, been good to me; he's not a fucking wonder-horse like some people think, but I suppose he's the best we've got. None of the rest of us are really going to set the world alight, but there's a chance he just might do some good with himself.

16

WEDNESDAY 7TH JUNE

Shite, shite shite shite day. Maths Paper Two and I blew it right out of my hole. I think I did reasonably well in Paper One, but Two was bloody impossible. I need to get an A2 or B1 in maths; it's the worst subject I've got. I need to get two A1s and an A2/B1. If I don't get the A2/B1 in maths I could have seriously fucked things and need to go through this mad clearing system they have for the English colleges.

One bloody exam, one exam and the whole thing's fucked.

Some of the younger girls at school think I'm a bit of a 'personality' because of the radio station and two of them ran up to me giggling and pointing after the exam. Younger girls have done it before, probably because I'm a little bit 'famous', if that is the right word, in this town. Though these days it could be because of the whole virgin thing. Either way I just told them to feck off, which I really shouldn't have done but I was just so pissed off and didn't want to deal with them. I want to go to the pub but I've got the final Economics exam tomorrow. I'm such a fecking eejit.

You build up your whole two years to these points, these sets of three hours, and you feck it like the moron you are. Jesus if I don't get these I'll either have to repeat next year or go to a shite college, which means no London, and the plan is fucked.

This is the plan loosely sketched out:

18–21: LSE college, part-time work at a radio station
21–23: Grad trainee at radio station
23–27: Own show on local radio station
27: Own show on Radio One England or big commercial station, then TV, then everything.

See and if I fuck this exam, it throws the whole thing out. Arse arse arse, so now it's going to be:

18–34: Repeat, fail again, get shitey job in hotel, and live in Clifden for the rest of my life known as 'The boy who couldn't leave town'.

And during that time I'll watch Michelle marry Liam and have beautiful kids and crush my heart on a daily basis, while I take up drink and die an alcoholic virgin at thirty-four.

That's just one exam, and my life has been ruined.

There was a plan, there was a proper-proper plan and

now it has all gone to shite. I'm the only one of the guys I know who actually has a plan. Maybe the others do and they're just keeping it secret. I haven't actually told anyone my full plan either but I'm pretty sure they haven't got one; they are just going to let life happen and see how it goes. Davey sure as fuck hasn't got one; not that it matters as I'm going to end up in the same place. Shit I'll probably end up washing dishes for him.

What's the saying? 'Life is what happens when your plan is a load of fucking rubbish and you're too thick to pass a poxy exam.' Very poetic.

I went for a walk, a long walk. I walked down to the sea for a bit. It's hard to be angry when looking at the sea but luckily I have the skill to still manage it. Eventually when I was a bit calmer I turned and walked home.

I saw Liam on the way back. He was walking into town from the garage where he works.

He was wearing his dark blue overalls and had a black T-shirt underneath and was walking like a fecking eejit, all big strides and Johnny Big Bollocks. Oh I'd love to give him a whack, just to see the look on his face, but then he'd get to see the look on my face of panic and regret as he proceeded to set about me. Look at me getting off on the idea that I could physically best him: I'm pathetic.

He walked past on the other side of the road. I don't think he saw me. I'm not doing the radio station at the moment: I set it running in the morning and that's it. I don't do lunchtimes and don't do afternoons; my head is so full of all these bloody facts that I'm trying to keep floating around the mush soup that is my brain. I had a dream the other night that all the information had leaked out of my ear and it was on my bedroom floor and I had to soak it up with a towel, wring the towel into a jug and pour the jug back into my ear. That's not a good sign, is it? Having said that, I also had a dream I was pregnant and gave birth to four dachshunds, which is probably more worrying.

Armies make people into killing machines. School has made me into a fact-memory machine. I wonder if anyone at school will kill themselves with the pressure; surely some poor sod will sooner or later. A guy in our year is on beta blockers to calm him down. That's a course we should have with the others we have at school: a calm-down course, maybe meditation or something so we enter the exam hall in a Zen-like state of serenity. They should have had that when we were younger too, before the feckin eejits who ruin the classes for others left: teach them to calm down, or failing that just hypnotise the little shits, so they sit there in the class and don't disturb the others. I don't know why they don't do that: no one would get hurt, and teachers would be protected if they could just learn how to do it. Imagine at those rough schools, when pupils attack teachers, the teacher could just click their fingers and say 'And SLEEP!' and they'd be safe. One for the notebook.

Anyway I haven't really got time to devote to the station at the moment. I turn on my portable radio at lunch to check that the signal is working. Also I told the listeners that I would be off for a few weeks with exams so they know not to write in or text anything as I won't be there.

I got about twenty good luck cards which is really sweet, and also a little unnerving, as I've never given my physical address out on the station, but then we are in the phone book so I don't think it would take too much digging to find it out.

I suppose the only plus side is these are supposed to be the hardest exams ever, or the biggest leap. I bloody hope so, I'm sick of them. Still I've done twelve: just three more to go and I'm a free man for the summer. I try to think philosophically about it: that beforehand if I knew I would only balls one up I'd have been happy. Hopefully that will be the only one.

But I can't help the feeling that the exams are eating into my brain; they are everything that is in my head now. The facts have squatters' rights; they are occupying as much room in my head as they like. They are an invited cousin who has taken liberties and it feels like I am now in *their* house. The part of my brain that controls walking, talking, sleeping and being has locked itself in its own bedroom and is operating from there, while the facts make a mess of the place. I hope they tidy up before they leave.

I get woken at night by facts: by economic theory, by literary prose, by mean mathematic distribution and French words.

The only plus side of all this disturbance is it's helping me think less about Michelle.

17

THURSDAY 15TH JUNE

Davey's mum is ill.

He hasn't told me yet. I found it out from Ma who found it out from one of the women at the bakery.

She's seriously ill, cancer ill, not-getting-better ill. They found it two weeks ago. She's only forty-two; she smokes and has a rough smoker's cough but she's had that cough ever since I can remember.

I feel sick. The thought of Davey suffering is awful; it breaks me up. I know he's a bit weird for some people's taste, but he's a good person, he doesn't deserve this. I feel protective of him too: I try to look out for him, to make sure he doesn't get into too much trouble and to try to steer him to be doing the things he should be doing, even if he doesn't know it.

People talk about having the metaphorical tools to deal with situations, but no one ever says what these tools are. I haven't got them and there's no way Davey has; he's just going to have to cope as best he can when she passes.

Someone is going to need to look after him: his family is a fucking mess at the best of times and this is just going to tip it all over. His mum was the one thing that somehow kept them all together.

I wonder if and when he was going to tell me. It's not something he'd just slip into a conversation, and he's not the best talker. I saw him Saturday; he might've known then or he might have only just found out in the last couple of days too. I wonder if his mum kept it from him. He's not one to pick up the phone, so I might have to give him a shout and let him know that I know. Maybe he doesn't want me to know and was going to tell me in his own time. Christ I really am narcissistic, his mum's got cancer and I start thinking about when he should have told me.

Ma didn't say how long she's got left, but I got the impression it's a not a year or a six-months thing; if they can't do anything for you it's basically a countdown. Cancer's a real bastard isn't it; someone you know is pretty likely to get it at some point and then you have to watch their eventual decline.

Ma's decided to step in and help out. She doesn't know them that well but knows Davey through me. With Davey's family everyone is a bit wary of them and so I never really see his mum with any friends. I don't know if they are close with anyone else.

I haven't seen his mum in a while. I tend not to go round their house that much even though me and Davey are such good friends; I think he's a bit embarrassed about the state of the place. It's pretty run-down and a real tip sometimes, and much as he's pretty carefree, I think he feels a bit ashamed of the way it looks: that's why he always comes to our house.

Ma said she's going to go round and see his mum tomorrow and see what can be done: maybe some cleaning or cooking, just check if she can help out in any way or make sure that there are other people like family who are going to help out.

Ma's good like that; she's a giver in this life. I'm worried this narcissism streak means I'm a taker or at best just a bit self-obsessed. But Ma will always give; maybe I didn't always notice as she's me Ma and you come to rely and expect it in a way, when I suppose I shouldn't.

I try to think of what I can do to help Davey. I might take him out for a pint tomorrow and get him smashed. I should do it tonight but I've got another exam tomorrow so I can't risk it. After tomorrow's exam I've got two days free so I can do it then; I'll still take it easy mind but I'll try to get him to talk about it and maybe open up.

I Google 'lung cancer' to see what I can find out about it. It's depressing as hell and I stop reading after the second article. There's not really a lot I can do for Davey, bar try to be a decent friend and let him know we're all here to help.

But the poor lad: what would I want to happen if it happened to one of mine? There's a one-in-three chance so it probably will get someone I care about in my life.

The nearest big hospital is in Galway so I imagine she'll have to go there but not yet; she's still fine to move around, if a bit wheezy. I definitely won't be able to look at her if I have to go round. How could you look at someone knowing what you both know? I wonder if doctors just get immune to seeing people dying.

The following day was English Paper Two in the morning and it went so-so. The funny thing about all this news is that I've stopped worrying about my exams for the moment; I truly am a narcissist. I give Davey a call early at 2.30 p.m. His lunch shift finishes shortly after then and he has time to go home and rest as he's also got an evening shift today starting at 5 p.m.

In my head, I'd been practising the 'Hello . . .' into 'I heard you had some bad news . . .' part since the exam finished. He didn't sound too bad actually. We agreed to meet up and have a beer after his work finished, which was around half nine unless the kitchen got hit really badly. The good thing about the American customers is that they like to eat early.

I waited in the hotel lobby for him to come out, which he did around quarter to ten, then we hit the Harp and drank at the bar until closing. We skulled four pints of Guinness in an hour which is decent going especially for me.

I don't really like Guinness. I drink it because I know eventually one day I will like it. I haven't told any of my friends that I don't like it yet. There must be something to like about it as why would everyone drink it, other than to get drunk, because there are other drinks that will get you drunk too.

I don't like beer either. Out of the two I dislike them equally but I kind of think Guinness is cooler and there is some vague nutritional benefit to it, whereas beer is just pissy sugary water that tastes bad, so has no plus side to it other than the alcohol.

Also I don't want to be a beer drinker. I want to be a Guinness drinker. I don't know why this is. It could be the endless advertising: I have been told that I want to drink Guinness enough times in enough Guinness ads and so I do want to drink Guinness. Da told me he didn't like Guinness until he was twenty-five and is surprised I like it so young. I didn't tell him I don't like it, as I think my drinking of Guinness is one of the things that impresses him about me.

It's strange to want to like a product and even though I don't like it, I still persevere with it in the hope that I will change. That must be what people are like with smoking: part of them wants to like it even though the first smokes are always awful. That's clever stuff to make you go against your natural instinct and persist until you are hooked.

I would smoke: I think it would suit me and I think I would look good with a cigarette, but the overwhelming feeling I would have every time I smoked was that I was having the piss taken out of me by the cigarette people. Like a big group of wankers in double-breasted suits laughing round a boardroom table.

To be fair with Guinness, I like it more once I've had a couple of pints, but then I like everything in the world more once I've had a couple of pints, apart from being quiet and talking sense.

This is the other thing I'm trying to perfect.

I think my teenage years are being spent trying to get good at stuff; I'm trying to get good at drinking. In my early teenage years I was aware that I should really try to get good at fighting, as I'm going to have to maybe be called upon to do it once in a while. I should also try to get good at sport but seeing as that is pretty much out of the question I don't worry about it. I want to get good at dancing, like be a cool dancer, but there's nowhere I could practise and if I ever did and got caught I'd get bloody crucified, so on that front I'm just going to go for enthusiasm over coolness.

Anyway I want to be good at drinking. I want that first taste to be as lovely as people say it is. Sometimes I'll take a glass, watch it settle, hold it up like people do with wine looking for something. I'll then take a gulp and let out a satisfied 'Ahhhhh' like I've just solved the final clue on a crossword. People will think that it has hit the spot, but I'm just a fraud. Out of the four of us usually drinking together there's got to be one if not all of us that doesn't really like it. I look for flinches in their eyes when they first taste; it just seems a bit bitter to me, you know?

Anyway four pints in just over an hour is pretty good for me even if it is that stuff.

We didn't talk about his mum once. I figured if he wanted

to talk about it he would, or we'd get drunk and he'd eventually break down, he didn't.

We went back to his and had a couple of cans and watched the telly. I was worried about bumping into his mum but the drink took the edge off that. She was upstairs in bed when we got back and she called down to check it was him coming through the door. After a bit she slowly came down the stairs to see who he'd brought home. I said hello to her and smiled. She looked a bit weird as I think she was wearing a wig; her hair was never usually that straight.

She said goodnight and went back up one step at a time. Eventually Davey fell asleep on the sofa. I left quietly and walked home. I think I did the right thing; I don't need to push him to talk about it until he's ready or unable not to.

18

Our town has a mentalist; I mean other than Davey. I'm led to believe each town has a mental.

Dublin has lots of mentalists. I think they get their own districts in cities that size.

We just have one: his name is 'Baahh'. Everyone calls him that; that's not his real name of course, it's just all he ever says. Any question to him is met with a 'Baahh'.

He stinks of piss. I would like to talk to him more but because of the smell I'd rather not.

He's not an alkie though, he doesn't stink of booze at all. I've heard tourists mumble stuff about him being drunk as they pass but that goes to show what they know.

He's smelly and scruffy but he's not pissed; he's not even a vagrant as he has his own house apparently.

The guards like to move him on in the summer as they think he gives the town a poor image. Every town has got to have a mentalist and I think it's good that our one is reasonably nice and not drunk and violent like some could be.

I sometimes wonder what he's thinking, if he's happy

in his role in life. I wonder how he slipped into the role: was he always mental or did something happen to make him mental?

Was he sporadically mental and then became full-time?

I wonder if he's ever been sectioned. We could make him into the town's celebrity. I should write this down: instead of exiling him we should take him closer to our hearts. Would that just be totally cool or what? Or would that be exploiting him for our own amusement? I'm not cool if we did it like that.

People used to laugh at the loons in the old days. I don't want to do that, but then would anything I do make any difference? Is he that far gone that he wouldn't notice?

I've never seen him smile, but having said that, I've never seen him upset other than with seagulls.

I wonder what social services do about him; I'm sure they're aware of him. I could speak to Doctor Kilpatrick but I'm sure there is some sort of doctor/patient confidentiality, even with mentals.

It's nice but sad to see him and what his life is, but what can you do? He's a proper face of this town but doesn't seem connected to it and it's unlikely anyone will do anything about it. I mean it's unlikely I will do something, which is wrong and I know it's wrong but I'm still not going to do anything.

And this is a small town. I can understand people in a big town not caring but we are a small town and people will care but only so far. I suppose people aren't going to care at all once I get to London.

I guess he just fell through the cracks. Maybe I could do something on the station to help him, use what small power the station has to get support for him, try to do something for the greater good. He might be beyond help; I mean it will probably fail but it's worth a go and worth a fail, even maybe if it makes things just a bit better for him.

Maybe I'm just naive; maybe when I'm older I'll harden to life; maybe London will make me harder, I don't know, but right now I want to do something to help the guy.

I feel bad for the mentally ill though: that probably sounds patronizing but I do. I think it will do for me at some point. I don't always seem to have the best of grips on my brain at this age; I can easily see it going off the rails at some point. At the moment with all the exam stress I can easily see it handing in its notice and moving on.

If one day my brain does go wrong I hope someone is going to help me when it happens.

I hate Manic Street Preachers. I've never really known why but I think it's mainly down to the fact that they are shite and James Dean Bradfield is a twat; so far that is all the evidence I have.

Regrettably 'Motorcycle Emptiness' is a brilliant song, but I can't let that get in the way of my opinion.

19

I'm a logic-based individual. I should logically be able to get Michelle, I should. There are only two things I need to do: make her not like Liam and make her like me. It shouldn't be too hard; I'm cleverish – I should be able to do this. He's a tit as well, so highlighting this shouldn't be too hard. I'm sure her friends have pointed this out to her too.

I've started running as well. Not many people run in Clifden; it's either windy or raining or both. People go for walks around here but they don't go for runs. They don't cycle much. I wanted to go for a run, just to prove a point and also to think. I'll think better when I'm running; when I'm doing something else my mind works best on other problems. When I stare at problems I can't see them; can't solve them, it's like those bloody magic-eye things. I can't do them either but it's the moment when you are not looking at it that you're supposed to be able to see something.

Why am I not able to see this? Actually, why am I bothering, am I just torturing myself because I know I can't have it? What if this is just a bloody crush and not the full-on crashing love that I'm pretty sure that it is? Christ if it gets worse than this I don't want to know.

I should stop thinking; thinking does nothing but paralyse me. No wonder alcohol is the number one choice of pastime in this country. It stops you thinking, or only allows you to entertain one thought at a time, which you've forgotten about by the time you open your mouth to say it in the first place.

I don't like that Amy Winehouse for doing a cover of the Toots and the Maytals song 'Monkey Man'. I'd like more people to know about the Maytals but at the same time I want them to be my secret or our town's secret, as I am a selfish music snob. If everyone finds out how great they are then our town won't be special to them.

20

THURSDAY 29TH JUNE

'Good morning Clifden, howareya? You well? Great stuff. Today is a special day today. Today I am eighteen years old. I am a man. I can legally drink. Big thanks to all those pubs that have been breaking the law serving me the last couple of years: it has been much appreciated. Let's keep it our little secret.

'Today on the radio station I'm going to play only tracks that I like, so no, Mrs O'Dowd, there's going to be no Take That for you today. I'm not going for any nosebleed techno but it might be some stuff you've not heard of before so please indulge me. This evening I'm going to be getting drunk at the Harp; if you want to buy me a drink that's where I'll be with the lads. For those of you who don't know what I look like, I'm about six foot one, built like a whippet with a quiff.

'Right, first up we're going to start with a little bit of ska from Mr Harry J. and his Allstars and this is "Liquidator".'

I've got loads to be getting on with this morning. Ma woke me up with a cup of tea and a pair of the most pristine trainers you've ever seen. Adidas Stan Smiths: honestly, they are killer; they look like my feet are smiling; I can't fail to walk good in them.

Sean got me a football, even though he knows I'm rubbish at it, and Fiona got me three golf balls but I've no idea why; I don't even play golf. The middle child is always the one that goes strange apparently; I need to keep a closer eye on her.

It sounds retarded but I've been so excited about my birthday that now it's here I don't know what to do; it feels like the day is dripping away already.

I've got to go into town to pick up a prescription for Ma, then I was going to go down to the hotel as Davey said I could have a free lunch on him and he'd cook it. I'm not sure I want to eat anything he's cooked, but he was so keen to do it, in the end I had to say yes.

He says he's learning stuff every day, and he'll do something really good for me. The lads in the kitchen listen to the station while they're prepping before service, so hopefully they'll treat me right and not gob in my food.

I've got phone calls to make regarding the speakers and the mixing desk I'm hiring. I've also got to confirm the band's rooms at the hotel but I'll do that before lunch.

I've got this massive checklist of things I need to do for the gig. I originally wanted it to be open air, as that would be so cool, or down by the sea, but you know what Connemara's weather is like; there's only about four days a year when it doesn't rain. It's why it's so green and why the cows taste so lovely but it does mean that I couldn't do it outside. There isn't a town hall or venue big enough so I'm hiring like this big-massive tent for the bands to play in. We're going to stick it up on the school fields.

Toilets. Christ I forgot toilets: I scribble down 'Toilets'. I should get some portaloos or something, but then I wonder if the school will let us use their toilets. I don't suppose they'd want a thousand people traipsing through their school, or we'd need to put in security to make sure things weren't broken.

The school has been unreal about it all. All they ask is that there are some charity bins for people to put cash into for them, and that they can have a stall selling food to make a bit of money. They did think about charging me, but when I told them this thing isn't costed to make any money they let me off. Although I do have to pay the electricity bill for August for anything above and beyond what last August's bill was.

And as for the bands: man that's hard work to get it all in order.

With the Maytals I managed to get them at half their usual festival price, but I had to beg for it. I had to make them fall in love with the idea of coming and then say that we couldn't afford to pay them their usual rate.

I did tell them this wasn't a profit-making operation and it was a community project. To get them to come took a month of begging and pleading.

I wrote a letter to Toots himself courtesy of his manager and included a DVD that I filmed.

I wrote:

Dear Frederick 'Toots' Hibbert,

Please allow me to introduce myself. I run a radio station called Radio Clifden in Clifden, Connemara, on the Beautiful West Coast of Ireland. It is a wonderful place as you can see from the postcards I have included with this letter.

What I need to tell you is that this radio station, and this town, loves Toots and the Maytals: we can't get enough of you. Every day we play one of your songs on the station and we get many messages about how much we love you. And the last song of the week is always 'Country Roads'.

I've also included a DVD with this letter. It shows just a selection of the people in this town who love you. [The DVD was a montage of clips of Connemara interspersed with people from all over town singing Maytals songs. Everyone I could get across town, including a selection of people getting the numbers wrong to '54–46 Was My Number'.]

Why I'm telling you this is that we are putting on an end-of-summer show and we would love it if you could travel to this town and make our year.

Yours sincerely
Lex Donal
Radio Clifden

I wrote another two letters to follow it up to show we were serious and professional. I even made up headed paper and everything.

We were dead lucky, and I mean so, so jammy-lucky. They were doing shows across Europe in the summer at festivals. Their final gig was on August 28th in Düsseldorf. Our day was September 2nd so they organised a show in London during the intervening week and one in Dublin on the Friday to fill their time before they got to us. They were then going to fly home from Shannon to NY to Jamaica the next day.

I couldn't believe it, and do you know it was Toots himself who phoned up to talk about it. His manager had shown him the letters and the DVD. When his rasping voice called up I had no idea who it was, and as soon as I found out I just started shaking. The guy is over sixty-five but he's got the body of a boxer; he's in better shape than me and I'm forty years younger. I've seen clips of them live and he still jacks around the stage like a bleedin' lunatic. The original Maytals are gone and now most of the band is made up of members of his family. Anyway he called wanting to know about our town, where we were and what we do.

I didn't tell him the radio station was just me in my bedroom. But I said I owned the station and was putting on the event.

People love to be loved, and I think the fact that he had a town he'd never heard of and never been to that was in love with him and his sound made him want to find out more.

I came off the phone and I had to tell someone, so I told everyone.

'*Listen up, folks,*' I said into the microphone, cutting off

Tina Turner mid song. '*This summer could be a very special one, I can't say much at the moment but I'm hoping we're going to be able to have our own festival this year for the people of Clifden, and ladies and gentleman I've just come off the phone with a major international recording artist who is very interested in coming over and playing for you.*

'*All I can say is that I'm so excited that I think my head might fall off. I want to be able to give you a massive present before I go this summer. You've all been so good to me I want to give you something back.*'

We hadn't talked money, we hadn't talked logistics, in fact all we had talked about was the town and all Toots had said was he'd think about it, but that he was interested. Sweet Jesus if I could pull this off it would be deadly.

My favourite track of theirs is 'Johnny Coolman'. It's not that well known. It would have to be something like that, as I am one of those kind of people. It would probably have been '54–46 Was My Number' but a lot of people like that one, so being the snob I am I changed it, even though no one has ever asked me.

21

DA – MICHAEL DONAL

Lex is a good lad.

We've done well with that one.

22

Ma went berserk today. She's never gone berserk; she's got angry and shouted but she's never just lost it. I can't even remember her getting angry with me much since I've been fourteen. When she got angry before there was always that threat that she would really explode and today I think I finally saw what the threat we were scared of was.

Da must have seen it before, as he has always warned us not to make her angry.

It was me she went crazy at too; it was me at first, then it was just at the world. It wasn't even me that wound her up: it was Fiona's fault.

We were all sat at the breakfast table. I'd done the first bit of opening up the radio station, then came down. Fiona was asking Ma whether she ever considered a successful career. Ma replied that she thought raising us three was a successful career, and Fiona goes, 'No, no, like a proper-job career, like be a businesswoman?'

And Ma says it wasn't really for her.

So Fiona goes, 'But why, Mammy, why wasn't it for you?'

and Sean's got some toast and he's trying to do that beer-mat thing where you half put it over the side of the table and flip it and catch it in your hand, but the toast is buttered one side and he's got his head down by it and is trying to flip it but quickly snap at it and catch it in his mouth, and Ma is getting the fruit juices and the cereal and doing another round of toast.

And Ma says, 'Some women are good at the business thing and get those opportunities and others have other opportunities.'

And Fiona is not letting up and goes, 'But you're clever, Mammy, you could have been a solicitor or something.'

And Sean does the toast again but gets it wrong and it lands butter side down on the table. And he picks it up quickly, and Ma sees and takes a cloth and wipes the butter off the table.

And Fiona tells how she is going to be a businesswoman, and she will get a nanny to look after her kids.

And Sean does the toast again and this time he gets it in his mouth and takes a bite, then he rotates it ninety degrees so he's got the whole length of the slice to flip again. And I finish my cereal and I shake the empty orange juice carton on the table and ask, 'Why haven't we got any more juice on the table?' and I meant to say, 'Have we got any more juice?' not, 'Why haven't we got any more juice?' It just came out wrong and I realise that it came out wrong and then Sean gets the toast flip wrong again, and Ma just turns on me.

She grabs my T-shirt, and starts pushing and pulling me

and saying, 'BECAUSE WE FUCKING HAVEN'T', and back-hands a glass off the table.

And Fiona starts bawling, and Ma tries to calm herself down and says sorry but then leaves to go upstairs. So I get the dustpan and brush out and tidy up and tell the other two not to say anything to Da.

23

SATURDAY 5TH AUGUST

So Ma must have said something to Da, as Da has decided to take Ma away for a night. Give her a break from it all. I think her going crazy the other morning might have been the jolt he needed to do it.

There's this new hotel in Galway called the G. It's very posh apparently: it has got spas and everything, got fancy food, fancy rooms. I'm not sure it's Ma and Da's style but I think the idea of a spa and a treatment for Ma is what sold it to Da. He can treat her to a nice meal, they can have a bit to drink and just go upstairs all in the same place. I think she needs a break; I think they both need a break. They've never been away without us.

They don't treat themselves that much. I mean we are not a rich family but we're not that poor, but I'd say Da is sensible with his money rather than tight.

He probably realises with this treat that if he didn't spend the money now on something for Ma he's going to have to spend a lot more in the future paying for replacement crockery and windows.

Anyway they set off just after ten in the morning to drive to Galway. It's up to me to look after Sean and Fiona all day.

Ma has done a tea of lamb pie for us that I just need to heat up, and there's enough bread and fillings in the fridge for lunch. I've just got to make sure they are in and don't get into trouble. Tea being already done is a shame. I could have gone to see Michelle and got sandwiches for us. Although on Saturday there's a greater chance of running into Liam, as he doesn't work Saturdays and in the summer he's not playing football during the day so he sometimes hangs out there. But I know for a fact it makes Michelle feel embarrassed; she always looks awkward when he's there.

I know it's wrong to know both their whereabouts at all times and I'm not stalking them or anything; I just pay attention to things and use common sense.

We wave them off in the morning; as they pull away the three of us walk back into the house. Sean goes up to his room; Fiona goes to the phone to call her friend but I grab her first. I tell her that Ma and Da going away for the night is all because of her upsetting Ma. I tell her Ma does a lot for all of us and she should appreciate it a bit more, but she pushes her arm free of my hand and runs off with the phone. I go to the kitchen to make some tea then take it back upstairs to my room.

I set the station going in the morning. The hard thing

with the station is that I put it on every day and some days I really fancy it and other days it has become a bit of a chore, like I fancy going into town or something. But it's a bit hard on the listener not knowing when you are going to be on and when you're not: that is, assuming they are tuning in to listen to me rather than just listen to the music.

I did an hour this morning; I've set enough songs going that if I can't be arsed to go back to it it'll be fine. I think I'll do a bit at lunch then do a bit in the evening.

Fiona lets me know that Mary is coming over, which is going to mean the house is full of noise. I can see Fiona being a lawyer when she grows up: she's got no problem talking. She's argumentative as hell and she's a pain in the arse; aren't they the main lawyer qualities you need? And she's bright, annoyingly bright.

When she is older and gets married she is going to take a perfectly decent man and she is going to destroy him, and Da will have to look that guy in the eye at the wedding reception and never say a word.

Mary comes round with more of those bloody magazines: honestly, some of them are nigh on pornographic. Ma tells them off sometimes about reading them and I can see why; there's no need to know all that stuff at that age.

Sean comes downstairs with his ball and tells us he's going to go play football with his mates. Sean's good at football; it seems to come a lot easier to him. I'm not saying the thick/good-at-sport thing is at play again; I'm just highlighting it when I see it. I'm not saying there's a cause and effect but I'm saying there is a correlation; Jesus, maybe those maths lessons will help me in the real world.

He goes out; Fiona goes upstairs with Mary to read 'How to know if a man is a commitmentphobe' or '431 great looks for this summer'.

I go to the living room and watch the box.

At lunchtime Fiona comes down with Mary when I call them. I make them a salad sandwich, and make sure when I cut theirs that I don't use the same knife I used to cut my ham sandwich.

They are currently in the habit of buying bottled water. There are five mini bottled water bottles in the fridge. You are not going to get much purer tap water than what we have here, but she insists that it's bottled water. Ma takes the cost of the bottled water out of her pocket money, but she still won't stop buying it.

So she cares deeply about the environment, she tells everyone; won't eat dead animals, but will drink bottled water in plastic containers, driven from miles away using petrol.

I can't be bothered to lay into her for being a hypocrite; I'm not sure she knows what one is. She will do soon, but today is not the day to tell her, and not in front of her friend.

Sean doesn't come home for lunch. He's probably still in a five-hour game of football; he'll either forget to eat or one of his friends' mothers will sort him out.

Fiona and Mary go to watch a soap opera and giggle. I go upstairs to the computer and chat into the mic a bit.

There are a few texts and emails that have come through today. One text says, 'U still a virgin? LOL.'

Every time someone does something like that it still gets me, like a little punch in the stomach. If ever I do get on a public radio station I suppose people will know about me and I haven't got a thick enough skin to cope with that at the moment.

At present there are five bits of graffiti in town where it says PMLV.

One in paint on the wall behind the Super-Value, just such a prime spot for Michelle to see every day and remind her what a sap I am. There's one again in white paint on the corner of Galway Road and Hospital Road: it's low down so you could miss it but I never do. There also a couple of bits on billboards, again both on the Galway Road going in and out of town: in the bottom right-hand corner of the toothpaste poster it says in big marker, 'Brought to you by the PMLV', and there's one further down the road saying, 'PMLV – OUR GOAL IS YOUR HOLE'.

Like, how mortifying is that to see it every day. To know that although not everyone knows what it means, there's going to be some people reminded every day; a small part of their day will be, 'Wonder if that wee Lex boy has had a ride yet.'

That's got to chip away at you. It really gets to me.

*

I do a bit more stuff on the radio in the afternoon. I do a phone-in during the afternoon and I think it's a good one. So my question is, 'Who is the oldest person in Clifden?' And if you can get that oldest person to phone in I will give you a free ticket to the festival AND if you want I'll give a ticket to the old person too.

I've set aside ten tickets to give away from the station in promotions.

I was going to give away another ten on Galway Bay FM; they are like the big station of the area, and you can sometimes on a good day get it in Clifden, but I don't think they are going to want to deal with a pirate station. They'd probably be pretty pissed off with me for asking and might make a complaint about me.

I always fancied a go on that station. When I come back next summer I might give them a try for a placement, unless they have the hump with me. They might not even know about me: I mean I'm pretty harmless and it's not like I'm a threat to them, but y'know what they are like with pirates; I think it's more the principle.

So anyway the 'Clifden's Oldest Person' phone-in starts. It works well as we get calls in straight away, and I take them live on air but man it's hard with the old people as they are pretty frail. You can't always hear them very well and they don't always make for the best personalities coming onto the show, as you want people who are lively and upbeat. It's not their fault, but some of them are hard work.

Mrs O'Dowd phones her dad, Joseph O'Dowd, who is seventy-five, and gets him to call up. He is confused by it all. When I ask him if he is OK to hold on while we wait for the song to end he asks, 'What song?' I tell him the radio station is playing a song, and that we are live on the radio station.

'Are we?' he says.

I try to do it quickly.

'Hello caller, can you tell me your name?'

'Joseph O'Dowd,' he faintly mumbles.

'And Joseph, how old are you?'

'I am seventy-five years old.'

'Thank you for calling, Joseph, you are in the lead with seventy-five years old.'

I fade him down, but in my ear I hear him say, 'In the lead of what?'

After him we get two more in their late seventies: Aileen Sheehan who was seventy-eight, then Mary Hogan who was seventy-nine.

Mary Hogan was good; she seemed quite sprightly for seventy-nine. She laughed a lot. I hope I can laugh like that when I'm that age. All my grandparents are gone, so I've never really known people that old and I don't remember them from when I was younger.

Mary Hogan sounded as if she could have made it to the festival. She didn't know there was a Radio Clifden or that there was a festival on but her granddaughter Kelly was with her and had persuaded her to call.

So then there's one song to play and Kelly is going to win the tickets if we don't get any calls until the end of the song. It's Phil Collins; it's bleedin' 'Sussudio', I mean talk about a shitebog record. Anyway I get a phone call, and it's all 'Hullo,' and I'm like, 'Hullo there, how can I help?'

And the guy says, 'I'm eighty-two,' and you can hear him breathing hard as he says it; he sounds like your man Darth Vader.

'Grand,' I tell him, 'and what's your name?'

'Eamon,' he says, 'it's Eamon Cosgrave. Do I win a prize?'

'Nearly, Eamon,' I say. 'Are you OK to stay on the line, then I'm going to stick you on the radio?'

He's OK, though his breathing sounds weak.

I fade the song out with still half of it left to play.

'Mary Hogan, I'm sorry but I think you have been beaten. We have a young fella on the line here, and he goes by the name of Eamon Cosgrave. Hullo there Eamon . . .'

'Ah hullo there,' says Eamon.

'Eamon, can you tell the people how old you are?'

There's a series of coughs.

'Eamon, are you OK?'

'Aye I'm fine,' he replies.

'Eamon, can you tell the people how old you are?'

'Yes, I'm eighty-two.'

'Eighty-two, folks, how about that?'

When I'm on the radio I sometimes find myself saying these rhetorical clichés like 'How about that?' and 'Are we loving that or what?' and I hate myself for doing it but sometimes they just slip out.

'So, Eamon,' I say, *'would you like the tickets for yourself or for a friend or a family member?'*

'I'd like them for my girlfriend,' comes the reply.

'Your girlfriend?' I say, a bit surprised. *'A girlfriend at your age, Eamon? That's good going, and what's her name?'*

'It's Stella Collins,' he says, coughing again.

I recognise the name, I think she might be one of Ma's older friends.

'That's no bother, Eamon, and do you mind me asking, since it's an age competition, how old she is?'

'She's eighteen,' is the reply.

And then I remember. Stella Collins is Doh's girlfriend.

And Eamon Cosgrave starts laughing, a young laugh.

I fade him down.

I fade up the next song.

I take out my mobile and text 'cunt' to Doh.

I left the station playing for the rest of the afternoon. I had been recording that section for my reel, so I could send it out to proper stations to show them what I can do.

Doh phones up after I'd texted him to laugh at me down the line. Stella is in the background clapping and shouting, 'Give it to me granddad.'

Pair of fucking retards they are.

I wind up the show at 5.50 p.m. I stick on 'Pomps and Pride' by the Maytals.

After shutting things down I go downstairs and stick the pie in the oven; it's just some leftover lamb in gravy covered with potatoes.

Sean comes in the door and his face is red and he hides

it from me and runs straight up to his room. It's probably because he's been running around all afternoon.

I stay in the kitchen and read the paper, but it nags at me that something wasn't right about Sean.

Eventually I give in to it and go up to his room to see him. Even from outside I can hear him sobbing.

'You all right Seanny?' I say, pushing the door open.

'No,' he says between sobbing. I can see he's grazed all down his left arm and his snot is running into his mouth.

'What happened man?'

'Patrick O'Shea is a cunt,' he says, still sobbing.

I've never heard Sean say the C-word before. I didn't even think he knew it.

'What happened?' I ask again.

He tries to breathe, sob and talk at the same time.

'Me and Connor are playing one-touch against the wall at the end of Beach Road, and Robbie McGrath comes and says "Pass", and wants to join in like and we didn't want to play with him, as he's two years older, and we didn't want him to join but he's there with Paul O'Shea, who's Patrick's younger brother, and Patrick is there as well. We says "No" and then Paul says, "He wasn't asking, he was telling."

'And Connor says "No".

'And I pick up the ball as we're just going to go home instead and then Patrick tries to take the ball out of my arms but I manage to keep it but then he shoves me over and then Paul takes the ball and gives it to Patrick, and Patrick gets it in his hands and like boots it over the cliffside and into the sea and he's a cunt Lex, and you can't do anything about it.'

And I feel sick.

I don't know whether he did it because he knew Sean was my younger brother, or just because he's a total prick, but what makes me feel even worse than them hurting Sean is that he's right: I can't do anything about it. I can't go and avenge him, which makes me pathetic, a feckin joke of an older brother.

I get out the antiseptic and wipe his arm up with it. I don't need Ma seeing it either, as she would go and do something about it, because she's not a hopeless coward, and her getting involved would just make me feel even more embarrassed. In the end I tell him to just wear long sleeves the next week or so.

After tea we sit in the living room in silence watching some shite TV.

Eventually I suggest Sean go get his PS2 and we bring it down and play it on the big TV in the living room.

I don't usually play computer games; they rob people of time and contribute nothing to the world. Think of the time people (mainly boys or boyish men) spend on those applications wasting their time: they're stealing the chance of learning or growing or just doing anything that could have a long-lasting effect that might leave us with something. I should start a campaign to stop people wasting their time doing nothing but getting better at a pointless activity. It's like sport all over again.

Women don't play games as much: could that be why

girls are racing ahead of boys at school, because the boys are being held back by being retarded enough not to break the lure of computers and their life-robbing temptations?

You could spend that time learning to play the guitar or any instrument or learn to cook or just do anything positive; it's not like you can achieve anything with a computer game other than completing it – win a competition or make money. Anyway all computer game competitions are won by autistic eleven-year-olds from Iowa.

It's not like it helps with hand–eye coordination in any other field than hand–eye coordination on computer games.

And besides it's not that the games aren't good because they undoubtedly are; some of the ones I've seen are amazing. It's just the games people play are so futile when computers can do so much more than just the games.

Anyway we end up playing Gran Turismo. Sean nails me at the start but eventually I get the hang of it, and through being a bit smarter in my driving I start to get the better of him. He just can't get the hang of corners; we'll do five laps of a circuit and he'll crash on the same corner five times. I'll crash the first time, maybe the second, but by the third I'll know to slow down on the approach.

Fiona complains she can't watch the big telly so goes to the kitchen to call Mary, who she has just spent the whole day with. Like what more could there be to talk about?

The English language is so limited because there are no words in it that could justify how much I hate EMO. Bands like My Chemical Romance are possibly the shitest of the shitest of the shite. If you really are going to make your living romanticising about death and suicide that much, at least show us you mean it by offing yourself in a vainglorious gesture of your own prick-ishness.

24

When I leave Clifden there's going to be no one looking out for Davey. It sounds soft but as I said before, people don't seem to get him. I don't really get him but I like him, always have. His mum is the one person he's genuinely scared of. His dad hasn't been about for years.

His mum has a lion tamer's control over all the kids, but Davey especially. I've never seen him stand up to or even question his mum. She is the frame on which that family is loosely pegged. If you think the boy is off the rails now, I am genuinely scared at the thought of him without his mum or me. It's a matter of time before the family implodes, and the caring part of me, which does exist, wants to stay here to make sure he's OK.

Ma has already spotted this and told me people have their own lives to lead, which is true but people are held up by the support networks around them. And when someone who is a bit fragile anyway has all of their support networks taken away at once, and you are taking one of those support branches away yourself, then it's very hard not to feel like you are doing the wrong thing.

Ma has said she will step in and make sure he is OK; she's scared I will let my opportunity slip if I stay.

The Mahons as a family are considered a little bit outsiders in Clifden. My ma went to see Mrs Mahon to talk about what she could do to help. Ordinarily my ma and Davey's mum speak now and again if they see each other out, but I wouldn't say they were friends. They know we are friends so that is their connection, but then I don't think Veronica Mahon has that many close friends. So Ma went round and sat at Davey's mum's bed for about two hours talking to her; I think she wanted her to know the support was there and that people would be keeping an eye out when she's gone. I imagine it would have been some chat, telling an acquaintance the things you would like taken care of when you're gone as you can't trust or don't like the family you have enough to tell them.

I don't suppose too many people imagine what their last few days on earth will be like, but for the majority of us it's probably lying in bed, our bodies in a shit-awful mess, waiting for the moment to come. It's strange we don't think about it more: dying has got to be the second most important moment in our life after getting born.

It's going to be heartbreaking either being here and watching it happen or being in London and imagining what is going on. I suppose this means Davey won't come over to London with me anyway; he'll need to stay behind for his family, but who knows, after a year or so when things get a bit more stable, it may be the kick he needs to get out of this town.

25

MONDAY 7TH AUGUST

I've been really trying to get my head down with the station lately; the exams are over so I've had a chance to really focus on it and get as professional as possible.

Summer's here and the tourists have all arrived. Clifden and the surrounding areas swell up to three times their population in the peak season. My favourite bit is when the weather starts getting better but just before the tourists arrive in May.

But I don't see them too much during the day as I'm in my bedroom and working on the station. It's bleedin' hard to fill a whole day on the radio station yourself: on a normal station you only do like three hours max at a time. I've been trying to do six or seven hours straight. There just isn't that much to talk about, so all it ends up being is me exiting out a track and intro-ing the next one. I suppose it's a bit smoother than the usual day when the tracks just run into each other; I fade them up or down. I only chat maybe once in every three songs.

I've also worked on trying to hit time marks, seeing if I can get it just right so that when the final track of an hour is just about to finish I've chatted enough before with the playing time to hit the news bang on the hour. Not that we have a news bulletin but it's something I should practise if I'm ever going to do it for real, and what better place than here where no one, or at least not many people, can hear my fuck-ups.

Presenters need airtime; it takes so much airtime to feel comfortable and most importantly natural doing stuff live on radio. The more time I can get in over this summer the better I should be able to get.

I've been trying to do sample CDs or 'Reels', as they are called, of a few songs and some links so that I can send them off to some stations. The student radio station at LSE sounds wicked, so I'll do some stuff for them and maybe one of the London stations would be interested. It might come to nothing but it'd be good to be on their radar all the same.

I've sent off three CDs so far, and other than the XFM I have heard nothing back. But the big benefit when recording myself and playing it back is I actually get to hear what I'm saying and how I'm sounding. I suppose it would be good to get some feedback to hear what other people, like a professional, were hearing when I was doing it.

I'm going to give the BBC another crack eventually. Their local stuff is a good way into places, but I kind of figure if I get shot down by them first time it's only going to make me gutted, whereas if I leave them until last I've always got something I'm working towards.

I've been trying to get more interactive with the audience, getting them to text in mainly or send in emails. I'm trying to do at least one on-air phone-in a day too so I get more comfortable with that.

Obviously I've been really pushing the festival and talking it up about what a great day it's going to be for Clifden. People seem genuinely excited about it and especially that Toots and the Maytals are going to be here.

When I haven't been working on the station I've been trying to finalise all the arrangements for the big day. Ticket sales have been going pretty well; I think we should sell out if it keeps up. People come up and talk to me in the pub about it and how cool it will be to have Toots and the Maytals here. Michelle has talked to me about it, which made me well happy that she was coming. Of course that probably means Dansey will be there too, but still at least she'll be there.

I'm torn between terror and excitement with this bloody festival. Occasionally I catch myself thinking this really could be a fantastic day for Clifden, a real memory to savour, but as soon as I find myself thinking like that I cut it out and go back to the usual me which is worrying endlessly about the things that could go wrong and the embarrassment I face if they do.

There is a big chunk of me that thinks I should never have started it in the first place and just slunk out of town when it was time to leave. But I suppose there's that other side, the side we've now established really is a narcissist, thinking what if I'm doing this as a grand big celebration of me? I mean I genuinely am doing this for the town. I had an idea, I thought I could do something good that people would like; I mean there's nothing wrong with doing that. You might think that I'm a show-off and there is definitely a bit of me that is, but this event is nothing to do with that. If I'd've had the idea last year I would have tried it then; it just happens to coincide with when I leave.

26

WEDNESDAY 9TH AUGUST

Davey's mum is dead; she died last night at 2.00 a.m. No one was around her at the time. She'd been in Galway County Hospital for six days. Davey had been going in every day to see her; he's taken time off work and apparently the chef has been all right with him even though it is peak tourist season.

He'd drive to Galway in the mornings, hang about town in the afternoon so others could see her without him and then sit with her some more in the evenings reading and watching telly. Then he would drive home at about 11.00 and then he'd come back in the next morning.

I don't know if his dad has been notified.

Davey's other brothers and sister were going in too, but Davey was the one who was doing the most time there. I didn't realise how close he was to her; I mean I knew he was scared of her but he never talked about her as if he liked her. I suppose the thought of losing her might've scared him into it.

I was giving him a call every afternoon to check on how he was. I asked if he wanted me to come along too for support but he said it was family stuff and she didn't want anyone else to see her as she was.

I can't imagine what it must be like on those wards. I wonder if they have specific cancer wards for people just waiting for their time to be called and gradually deteriorating up to that point; they couldn't do that, could they? That would just be too unbearable for anyone to actually work in a place like that, like a check-out clinic.

They thought she had at least another couple of weeks left in her so they hadn't been prepared to be there when it happened and she slipped away.

They called Davey's house at 7.00 a.m.; they figured there's no point in waking someone in the middle of the night and making them drive an hour to Galway at that time: what's done is done.

Davey was upset that she wasn't given the last rites; he's not religious but it mattered to him for some reason.

He called this afternoon at 2.00 p.m. to let me know. He's got to arrange a funeral whilst I am in the middle of arranging a festival. I Google 'how to arrange a funeral checklist' and forward the results to him.

Why is my response to any major event to ask Google what I should do?

I briefly thought about cancelling the festival. It's not going to feel right but it's still a few weeks away and although it sounds cold the dust should have settled a bit by then. Besides I could do something for Cancer Research or one of those cancer charities.

27

WEDNESDAY 16TH AUGUST

The day of the funeral for Davey's mum arrives. There is no radio station today and for the last few days I haven't talked on air; I have just loaded up some tunes, and tried to make sure there was nothing that might be considered in bad taste.

I'll probably start on again in a couple of days I think.

We were waiting outside the church when the hearse drives up with the coffin inside. It was just awful man, like it became too real for me. I mean that's his dead mum is in that box in there. I started to blub.

Inside the church I sit four rows behind Davey. I start crying again; I am crying more than anyone else in the church, which is bad. Every time Father Cafferty starts a new topic I start to cry again. It's getting really embarrassing but I can't stop it. Ma who is sitting next to me gives me a nudge to tell me to pack it in. Even Davey isn't crying; neither are his brothers or his sisters: it just seems to be me and I'm crying for all of them. I might be crying for me too, for the stress, for the leaving home, for the exams, for my friendship with Davey.

Davey is just staring straight ahead: doesn't once look at the coffin, doesn't look at Father Cafferty, doesn't look at his family, just looks through everything and forward. Some of my tears are selfish but most of them are for him. I just don't want to see him hurting, not that he's shown any sign of it so far. Without his mum means that's him without any guide now for the rest of his life, no one older than him to help him on his way; his brothers are no use and his dad isn't around.

There are some uncles and aunts in attendance but I don't know who is who; I don't even know the immediate family that well, short of being scared of both the brothers and even the sister. Davey never talked about the uncles, so I don't know how the family is made up.

Ten minutes into the ceremony and the door at the back of the church opens. Father Cafferty was doing a reading at that point, so it was quiet enough that everyone heard the door go. A few people looked round to see who it was and Ma was one of them; she turned back to the front and let out a 'Sweet Jesus'.

A man comes in; he looks about sixty, and looks like crap. He has grey-flecked hair which is barely there, and what is left is wet and undried against his head. He is wearing a long dark tatty woollen coat and tries to shuffle as unobtrusively as possible down the side of the church for a space to sit. There are no spaces down the side and no one moves in for him, so while Father Cafferty carries on and ignores the interruption he settles for just standing by the wall.

I saw Davey had noticed him and was no longer staring in front but was staring at him.

We rose for a hymn and Davey keeps staring.

'That's David's dad,' whispered Ma, as the organ played the intro.

There was no eulogy by a friend or family member; Father Cafferty did the whole service. After Davey's dad had come in I managed to stop crying for a while: it gave me something to focus on.

At the end of the ceremony people milled around outside the church, shaking hands and giving hugs, particularly to the children. I held back a bit from Davey and waited until he had a bit of space before getting to him. Every hug he receives he just stares ahead, immune to the good wishes. He scans the crowd, looking for his old man. I can't see him so maybe he snuck away at the end.

I am going to say, 'Let's go get a pint,' but I end up crying after saying 'Let's . . .' Out of the tears I stutter '. . . P-p-pint?' which seems to work as we walk off to the Harp.

The rest of the congregation sets off towards Davey's house where the wake is being held. We went in the opposite direction; we'll catch up with them after.

We walk to the pub in silence. The pub is empty of customers. Inside Davey takes a seat in the corner and I get two pints of Guinness from Michael.

'These are on me lads,' says Michael, loud enough for

Davey to hear. Davey gives a nod in thanks and gets back to staring at his table.

When the drinks settle I raise my pint and say, 'To your ma.' Davey mumbles, 'Ma,' and we clink glasses. We sit in more silence for a while, Davey staring at the table and me out the window, but it's not awkward; it feels warranted.

After ten minutes or so Davey says, 'Cafferty did good, no?'

'Aye, he did a grand job,' I reply.

'Funeral guys, they did a good job too.'

'Aye, very respectful.'

'. . . and the flowers,' he adds.

'She'd have loved the flowers.'

Lots more long pauses.

'She from a big family, your ma?' I ask.

'One of five: two brothers, three sisters, she was second eldest, the eldest girl.'

'They all there?'

'Most of them, I think,' he replied. 'Quite a few of the family, hadn't seen them for years.'

We skulled the first two drinks then Michael brought over another two, and put them on the table.

I didn't know if to bring up his dad as I didn't know how he'd react, but in the end it just kind of flowed out and he seemed fine with talking about it for a short while.

'That your old man there?'

'Yeah, that was a turn-up, hey? No one knew where he was so I don't know how he found out, or more to the point how he stayed sober long enough to get here.'

'You hear from him ever?' I asked.

'Not for the last seven years at least. Last we knew he was in Cork working as a shopfitter, but that was a long time ago.'

'He a nice guy?' I asked.

'Nope,' was the answer, and when I asked more, he cut me off with, 'Let's not talk about that arsewipe today, no? Let's just get drunk for my ma, hey? It's what she wouldn't have wanted.'

We were going to leave to get back to the wake after that one, but ended up staying for another couple; it felt the safer and easier choice.

After three pints I agreed that at the festival Davey could DJ in between the bands. I know it's a risk but at least he knows how to use the gear. I fully realise this is putting Davey in a position of trust, and that usually when people put Davey in a position of trust he abuses it and never gets asked again.

At school they had a day where they made some of the less well-behaved kids Prefects so they could see things from the other side and understand why Prefects and rules were needed. The Prefects ended up giving the kids in second year cigarettes and teaching them to smoke, and claimed that they couldn't be punished for this as they were Prefects and thus above the law. I think they thought it was like diplomatic immunity.

Anyway I couldn't turn him down on a day like today, but I did make sure he promised he definitely wouldn't play any techno or any of that bloody trance music he likes. At work apparently if they haven't got me on the radio, they play trance in the kitchen first thing in the morning, to liven them up and punish Chef's hangover. If there isn't a health and safety law to forbid Davey having trance music and sharp knives in the same place, there should be.

When we finally left the pub Davey was arguing with Michael that Roy Keane was a midfield cyborg and not 100 per cent human. I tried to join in but it's football and all I know is that he's Irish and he gets angry a lot.

By the time we left for the wake it was just shy of three o'clock. This is my first funeral as like a semi-adult and I'm learning today that funerals mean a day of long drinking and starting early, so when we got to the house things were moving already.

Davey was greeted like a son returning home from war, with bear hugs and pats on the back, and the mood was much more jovial than it had been at the funeral earlier.

I got talking to one of his aunts whilst an uncle put his arm around him and shouted in his ear.

One of the strangest things about the wake was they had decided to play some of the songs that his mum had liked which meant an awful lot of Carpenters songs, and a lot of awful Carpenters songs and the same ones over and over.

I need to be less bothered about music sometimes, but eventually I cracked after three hours and put on a Beatles' greatest hits CD. People were too drunk to notice by then, but it felt like a blessed relief.

An uncle or a family friend started dishing out the whiskey in the kitchen, which looking back was a huge mistake. I started arguing with the guy that Roy Keane was a cyborg and the best centre forward I have ever seen.

I'd not spotted Davey for a while, so when he walked past the kitchen door I dragged him in and made him tell the man why he was wrong about the thing I had been telling the man. The man grabbed Davey's shoulder and told him if there's anything he needed, anything, just anything, any-thing, anything, any-single-thing, to let him know. I whispered in Davey's ear, 'Ask him for a pony,' and then collapsed on the floor in hysterics. Davey and the man stared down at me and I had to apologise and crawled across the floor and into the sitting room.

I got talking to Jon, Davey's oldest brother. I always thought he had hated me and I was right, as he told me he had always hated me. 'Fucking-know-it-all-radio-dick-wank' were his exact words, but then I got the arm round the shoulder to tell me I was good for Davey and a good friend and all right by him, which was decent of him.

It was getting dark about nine-ish and I was sat on a sofa chair talking to no one, and nursing the brandy that I was now drinking.

Out of the front window I saw illuminated by the street lamps the slow-moving figure of Davey's dad. He stood at the end of the garden looking at the house for what must have been two minutes, then walked towards the house. The door opened and I don't know who was there but he turned back and walked away, not saying anything.

I headed back into the kitchen to find Davey. I didn't tell him about seeing his dad.

The last I remember I was in the back garden smoking. I hate smoking.

28

THURSDAY 17TH AUGUST – PART 1

I wake up on the floor of Davey's room, head on carpet between a chair and the base of his cupboard. My body is curled round the lower part of the chair. It is 6 a.m. and I am woken by a combination of Davey's breathing and the light that has started to come into the room. I am still utterly bollixed.

I decide to get up and get home before the hangover can start. I leave Davey's room leaving his still-clothed body on the bed and search for a toilet. I find one and then pee a liquid which most closely resembles marmalade.

As I get down the stairs I see there are still some people up in the kitchen. I hold up my hand to say hello and goodbye and head out home.

Got to drink some water: don't want to drink some water but got to drink some before I go back to bed so that when I wake up again hopefully it will take some sort of edge off the pain that is coming my way.

I push open our front door and Ma is unfortunately already up and in the kitchen.

'Jesus,' she says, taking in the shell that has presented itself; she moves her hand to her mouth.

'Bed,' I mumble, and go straight upstairs.

'I should think so,' she replies.

I try to use my curtains to cover any form of light coming from outside. I crawl into bed and realise I have forgotten my water. Fuck it, I will get it later.

THURSDAY 17TH AUGUST – PART 2

Oh sweet baby Jesus, why do you hate me? Why hast thou taken to punishing me so?

Pity has no equal to a man with a hangover bad enough to kill a whole forest. The mind is weak, it plays tricks; pity senses the weakness and tries to make a play. Oh how I hurt.

Ma hasn't even been up to see me; she would usually come and check. It is now 10.30 a.m. I am in for a hateful and hurtful day.

I should never drink whiskey. I don't like it, I don't like it and I don't like it. More so it brings a pain I cannot take. I try to go back to sleep and close my eyes tightly. It doesn't bring solace.

Fiona opens the door and brings light. Light hurts.

She says, 'Mammy says you need to go up to the school to get your results. She says that although they are your results we as a family have suffered enough for them and we're not going to wait any longer so you better get up.'

The results.

I forgot about the exam results. I knew they were today; Christ all summer I've been thinking about today but with the funeral and everything I'd forgotten.

Shite, now I've got to go and find out.

The school, I'll have to go up to the school and there'll be other people there, and honestly I don't think I can move.

Fiona is still stood in the doorway. 'Well?' she says, 'Are you getting up or what?'

Give me a minute, I say, and she closes the door. I can hear her shout 'HE'S COMING DOWN' as she runs down the stairs.

I put on jeans and a T-shirt. I open the door and mumble 'Fuck it' and head down the stairs.

'Do you want some breakfast first or shall we just get in the car and go?' says Ma.

'Go, go, go!' hops Fiona.

'Away,' I say, trying to shoo her back.

I get some orange juice out of the fridge, and drink it in two gulps. Both Fiona and Ma are watching me.

'Come on then, let's do it,' I say.

Fiona says 'Yes!' and punches both hands in the air.

'You're not coming with us,' I say to Fiona, who instantly turns to Ma, who looks back at me and it's done.

'Fine, you can come but you have to be quiet.'

Another 'Yes!' from her and she's handing Ma the car keys and opening the front door for us all.

In the car on the way I feel rancid: the car is hot, it's too hot, I'm sweating, which is the heat but also the booze but isn't the nerves. I'm not feeling nerves, just sick, and not nervous sick: nauseous, dehydrated, plague-ridden sick.

Ma knows better than to talk. Fiona is talking but fortunately to herself.

I get to the school and we drive in. People are milling round the main entrance and reception which is obviously where they are doing the results.

When she pulls up in the visitors' spaces Ma says, 'We'll just wait here for you. Come out when you are ready,' which I really appreciate.

I get out and walk towards the entrance. I know for a fact that I am going to be sick in the next hour.

I am just hoping I hold it until after I get the results, otherwise it will look like I'm a nervous wreck and I'm not: I'm a physical wreck.

Mr Maguire the headmaster is waiting just inside the main doors. He's an all right guy, and has been good to me with the concert and everything.

He takes a look at the state of me and says, 'Ah Lex Donal, I believe you are supposed to do the celebrating after the results.' I wince and say 'Aye' in the hope that he leaves me alone.

He goes on to tell me that if I go into the room behind the reception desk his secretary has our results. Once I get those I can then go down the corridor and see how my friends have got on.

'Good luck,' he says, and I know the bastard has seen

our results so he knows what I've got and it's probably the highlight of his fucking year to be in the position where he knows and he isn't telling.

I get into the office and Mrs Caskell is there. She looks up and smiles, then flicks through the box of envelopes until she gets to mine, and she hands it to me.

I open the envelope. Unfold the paper.

Alexander Gabriel Donal . . .

Business Studies – A1
Economics – A1
English – A2
French – B2
Geography – A2
History – B2
Irish – A1
Maths – B1
Physics – C1

I read it again.

Business Studies – A1
Economics – A1
English – A2
French – B2
Geography – A2
History – B2
Irish – A1

Maths – B1
Physics – C1

I need two A1s and an A2 or B1 to get the points.

I've got three A1s.

Three A1s.

THREE FUCKING A1s.

I DID IT.

I DID IT.

I DID IT.

I still haven't spoken yet.

Mrs Caskell looks at me with a hopeful smile that says, 'Well?'

'I did it,' I say softly.

Then I'm out of there, out to the front door, down the steps, when I hear 'Lex!' called, and I turn back to see Mr Maguire.

He sticks out a hand and says, 'Well done, lad.'

I say, 'Thanks, sir,' but am already letting go and sprinting across the playground to the car. Ma can see I'm smiling, so is opening her door, and Fiona is getting out the other side, and I get to Ma and she gives me the biggest hug and Fi comes round and hugs me too, but the sprint has caught up with me and that's the point when I'm sick. I try to make it round the back of the car so people can't see me.

It's a bad sick too; I end up on my hands and knees as I keep retching into a drain.

'That's disgusting,' is what Fiona keeps saying.

I try to tell her to get back in the car but am having trouble getting my breath.

Ma is on the mobile to Da; she's describing what is going on to him. She says, 'The good news is you have a son who is going to university; the bad news is he's currently ruining the reputation of the Donals by lying on the ground and puking himself sick.'

'Are you finished?' she shouts over the car.

'Think so,' I say.

'Would you like to walk home?' she adds.

'It might help sort me out.'

My karaoke song would be Candi Staton – 'Young Hearts Run Free'. I would murder it, though I don't know how it would sound to others, as I have never been to a karaoke bar and they are a bit thin on the ground in Clifden. Tonight though, it might be some overblown guff from Queen. Tonight I am going to be Clifden's very own karaoke bar.

So I'm walking back home, slow, and all I think is: I did it, it's done, I did it, it's done; it's done, and the work and the hours and the stress, it worked, it all worked, it all happened and happened right and this is it. It's on, London is on. London, I am coming.

I get back to the house just after 11.30; I get a glass of water then go back up to my room and lie on my bed.

It's when lying on my bed I remember that I haven't turned the station on. I turn on my mobile as I boot up the computer and there are fifteen messages and most have ???'s in them and 'Well?'

I turn the station on, mumble apologies and choose a previous day's music to go on but put the tracks in alphabetical order so it's different from that day. I turn the volume low and lie on my bed again.

'I did it, I actually did it.'

My first want is to tell Davey but I don't think it's the right time. I'll give Doh a call too to find out how he got on with his.

I'm more relieved than happy, though I am happy. I don't want a drink though, that I don't need today. I suppose people will be out tonight to celebrate. I might have something later on, but it's too early to think about it.

This is it though: I'm actually going to London. I'm on for this thing; I'm ready for it, but right now I'm ready for another lie-down.

29

SATURDAY 19TH AUGUST

Two weeks until the festival and we've finally sold all sixteen hundred tickets. Given that it is effectively more than half the town of Clifden in normal season, that is pretty good going. I phoned up the *Galway Independent* in early July and asked if they would do an article on us for their 'Living' section. They did, which was cool though the photo of me on the school field was pretty gormless and Davey takes great delight doing the two-arms gesture I'm doing in the shot whenever he can.

The two-arms gesture was to demonstrate where the festival was going to be. The photographer said the photo needed to show me showing the venue for the event, and as it was the school playing field it was me stood on the school playing field with my arms saying, 'Here's the school playing field.' Only now Davey and Doh like nothing better than to use their arms in the same way to say, 'Look here's your pint,' and 'Look here's your crisps,' all whilst pulling the same gormless face.

They did the article in return for me taking out a couple of adverts, one to go with the article and one the following week. It was hard to put it together because like I'm not a graphic designer or anything. Despite my occasional foray onto b3ta.com, it's hard to not make it look like some tacky jamboree thingy. I did all right with it but I still wasn't that happy.

I think about 200 to 300 or so people coming will be from the Galway area, a hundred or so from the Connemara countryside. I had tickets on sale at both Redlight Records stores and Zhivago Records so if you lived in the area and wanted to go you could buy them there. They all sold out eventually but it took a bit of time.

30

SATURDAY 19TH AUGUST – AFTERNOON

Have you ever had a situation where you thought if you couldn't hold it any longer and you broke and started to laugh, even though you were desperately trying not to, that once you started to laugh, you would never, ever be able to stop? You would wake up the next day and you would be silent for like three seconds, then you'd remember it again and then you would laugh non-stop for the rest of the day until you collapsed, and then you'd wake up again the next day and do it all over again. And this one laugh that you could never stop was all because that one time you broke and you let it go, because the thing you'd seen, the thing you'd heard, was just so funny that nothing could stop its progress.

And that is me now, that is what I am faced with; if I break into a grin I am finished. I am sat in my bedroom with Liam Dansey, y'know, 'Wanker Dansey'; I will come to explain how this happened later. We have the radio station running and are just chatting in between songs, like mates who hang out together would.

I'm trying my hand at interviews on air and as he's a sort of sports star of the area he is a good place to start; he wanted to come over and see the station too.

Liam has just told me, off air and very much in confidence, how misunderstood he is, as very few people get to know the real him because of his reputation and what is expected of him. He said that he doesn't really want to be a mechanic all his life, that he has hopes and dreams but he keeps these to himself. He's shy, he doesn't want anyone to know what he wants to do because he's scared they will lose respect for him, or worse, laugh at what he wants to do. But he's started to realise that if he doesn't try to do something about his dream then he's going to miss any opportunity he has of achieving it, and he thinks it's time to try something or give up on the idea and just settle for what he's got.

So I, his new friend, have become the person he can tell this dream to, because he thinks I am someone who can understand his situation: someone who has dreams himself, someone who doesn't always want to live in this town, and also he thinks maybe I am someone who can help him achieve that dream.

He hasn't even told Michelle this secret, that's how big a secret it is; it's only really recently he's got his head together and decided that this is what he wants to do. And what is it Liam wants to do? What is it that Clifden's central-midfield hard man dreams of?

Liam wants to sing; he wants to be a pop singer. He wants to be in a pop band or a boy band or a solo singer, but he wants to sing and maybe dance. He doesn't want to sound vain or anything but he thinks he is reasonably good-looking enough to try to do it; he thinks if they put together another Boyzone or Westlife, that's the kind of thing he's always wanted to be in. And he wants me to listen to him sing because like, 'I know about music and stuff so I'd be able to tell if he's like, got it or not,' and 'Maybe I could even go on the radio or something . . .,' because '. . . if I could build up a bit of a following in my hometown and do a few gigs then maybe that could like get some A & R men interested,' or 'If when I go off to London I could put him in contact with people who could help him get somewhere . . .'

Now am I a little bollix for wanting to laugh at his dream? Would you not burst out laughing? This guy is the only thing between me and Michelle, a man who up until a week or so ago I loathed more than anyone I knew. The only thing stopping me laughing until my ears fall off is just how desperate and fragile he looks while telling me this.

In my head I'm already telling this to Davey, Danny and Doh. I am already reeling back and basking in the glory of the greatest story I have ever told them in my life. I can see their eyes crave for more details about just what he said to me; should I tape this and get him to say it again? Could this really be true? Could I really be this lucky, that the guy I hated – though to be fair he's not as bad as I had expected and I will tell more about that later too – is laying before me his most bare secrets and ones that could destroy him if I were to let this laugh out.

I've always despised Boyzone and Westlife, that generic sterile pop, but now I have changed my mind about them. That Liam Dansey looks up to them and wants to be like them makes me think of all those bloody times I've had to listen to them, all the times Fiona has begged for them to be played in the kitchen, all the damage they have done to Ireland's international standing: it was all worth it just so it would allow my man Dansey to have his dream.

And what a shitey dream it is too, like if you're going to have a dream, have a fucking dream, not something as corny as this. So am I going to let him sing for me? Of course I am, because, as I hope we may have established so far, there is a part of me that is an evil little shitebag. I hope to improve this part of me one day but for the time being I'm learning to live with it.

So I turn down the speakers so there is silence in the room; the station is still playing, bloody Rod Stewart, and I can see that the music is still playing on the levels but I want to give Liam my undivided attention. Cruel? Only if I laugh am I cruel, but what if it is so bad I can't help myself? I was almost in pieces when he was telling about it all; for me to actually hear him sing out loud could be too much, I could break.

So Liam stands up, and I swear to God this is really happening, in my bedroom, and I am frozen by the possibility of what I am about to witness.

And he starts; he is singing and it is not Boyzone or Westlife but it is Take That and it is 'A Million Love Songs' and disappointingly Liam can actually sing, a bit, enough that it's not terrible. In parts it's actually not bad; he struggles at some of the big moments but to be fair to him he does really let go, waving his arm about and all, and he attacks the song. I did think afterwards I could have opened up the mike so everyone in Clifden could have had a listen on the radio, but I'm not that much of a shitebag. After a couple of minutes he finishes the song, and I don't know what to say. I genuinely don't know what to say; someone has just sung themselves out for you and it wasn't brilliant so I can't lavish him with praise, but then it wasn't terrible so I can't really say that, so what do I say? In the end I say nothing until eventually he asks, 'Well, what do you think? It wasn't any good was it?' and he's back to being all fragile again.

I'll tell you one thing about Dansey: aside from the singing the thing I couldn't help but notice is he's got muscles, like proper man muscles, like on his shoulders there's a chunk of meat that you could really see when he was going for it in the song. The muscles come out of his T-shirt and go into his neck; he's like a proper man, a proper unit. Me, I'm like a collection of bones with the lightest covering of skin and muscles to allow them to move.

He probably does weights and stuff; maybe I should do weights, maybe so when I did finally get naked with a girl I wouldn't look like some stretched cheese straw, all pale and gangly.

I bet he's got a six-pack too; I bet Michelle loves that. I bet Michelle rubs her hands all over his muscles and shoulders, because he's a man, a proper man, and sat opposite him it's clear I'm a boy, a long skinny boy, but definitely more boy than man. If I was a girl, like not sounding like a homo or nothing but physically I would definitely go for a manly man, like if you took away the brains and interestingness from me to even things up, you're going to go for him aren't you? That stuff about being funny, that's a load of crap; they say that so they don't sound shallow but it's not true. Look at Davey: he's funny, but no girl wants a bar of him. That said, Doh is funny, clever funny, and he's got Stella. But Liam's not funny at all; he's not said one funny thing since we've been friends this last week, but girls really go for him.

I decide I'm going to do sit-ups tonight to get a six-pack. I might start eating more, maybe bulk myself up a bit. I'm never going to be big, but at least I could stop being so scrawny.

Anyway, so back to my room and Liam. I tell him, trying to sound as professional and knowledgeable as possible, that he has got 'a voice' and that I was surprised how good he was. I say that for someone I am assuming has had no actual training, that was very good, and you have something that could be worked with to build it up. I start to talk about voice coaches as if it's something I am really up on, and I think I give a passable attempt at encouragement and helpfulness without going over the top or being unduly negative.

I mean, I actually don't know too much about music, not the technicalities. I love music; I know what sounds good and what doesn't, but the details like tone, pitch and key I haven't got a clue about. I tried to learn guitar when I was fourteen; it's still sat in the bottom of my cupboard. I just wasn't patient enough with it and my hands won't do what they're told, just like my feet wouldn't when I played football.

But Jesus, that was a weird moment. Fiona knocks on the door to ask what is going on. I think she just wants an excuse to see Liam. She's done everything she could to try to talk to him since he came in the house.

I think she is impressed that I know him. She wants to get her priorities sorted out.

We carry on with the station for another hour until I wrap things up. In between songs we talk about where he could go, or if he should try for one of those TV talent shows (I tell him I think they are bad news, that they are such a long shot and they just chew people up and spit them out and the only winners are the guys who run the show, but he quite likes the idea of them). He even does a couple of links towards the end of the hour which he gets all excited about. He does this one about his football team Clifden Rovers and gives a big shout out to them and says about how they are all are going to have to do pre-season training soon, and another shout for the guys at the garage who all listen to the station. Then he goes home as he's going out with his mates tonight; he says I'm welcome to join them but I pass it up. Saturday is 'lads' night', Friday is 'birds' night', so he says. They're going to get right on it, as it's one of his buddies' birthday. I can drink; not too great at it, but I can't stick it away like this lot; they'll demolish like twelve pints in an evening. I'd bloody drown if I drank that much.

Three reasons why I am better than Bono:

I am taller than him.

I have never made a shit record.

I am not an arsepipe.

So me and 'Nemesis' Liam, now 'friends'. Bit of a weird one that. Davey thinks I'm mad; I think that's a double negative, making me right, cos if Davey thinks something's mad and he's nuts it means it's sane, unless it means it's double nuts, or nuts squared.

Yeah, so it turns out Liam did know who I was, and that whole 'Ballbag' thing actually quite upset him. He sort of was aware who I was because of the radio station, and had generally thought I was probably all right until the 'ballbag' night.

We were outside the Harp; summer evening, beautiful day, it's still light even though it's like nine o'clock, and he comes right up to me, and I brick it because I think maybe he's going to get me back or he finally knows about all the Michelle stuff, but he doesn't.

He goes, 'Lex, right? The radio guy yeah?'

Before he goes any further I get in first and apologise for the other month. I had to tell him how much pressure I was under with the exams and I hadn't eaten that day and I had drunk too much and was a bit off my head. I said it was nothing personal.

He says it's cool; we're cool; but don't do it again or I'll knock you out, but like he says it in a jokey way, but he probably would.

Then he tells me how much he likes the radio station, and like does an impression of one of the jingles.

He says originally he thought I was a lot older; that I sounded older on the radio. He says the lads in the garage listen to it. In fact, and this is really weird given he's such a wanker and all, he came across like really nice and that, not what I thought he was like at all.

When he went back to his mates, Doh was all, 'What's that about? Are we going to have to get involved, cos his mates are big fuckers?' I was a little stunned. One, I hadn't seen him at the pub anyway – usually if I see him in a pub after last time I just move on; and two, he just came over and was really pleasant to me: Liam Dansey, Liam 'Arsehole' Dansey, Liam 'The Missing Link', Liam 'Knuckle-dragger'.

He came over again later in the evening for another chat. This time he was a bit drunker and he was nicer still: really weird, he tells me I should do it professionally, tells me he'd love to have a go. He asks me if he can come over, and I'm like, 'Yeah, sure' and I sort of meant it but I didn't; I just hoped he'd forget about it next day. And he gets me to come over to meet his mates, and Doh is right: they're big fuckers all right. And I can see Danny and Doh over one of their shoulders, and Doh is miming licking someone's arse. I have to look away so I don't laugh.

When I get back to the lads they ask me who my new boyfriend is and if I'm going to be playing 'ball' with the boys on the weekend, if I'll be flicking towels with them in the showers?

I try to play it cool like, but my head's spinning a bit, it was a bit of a trip you know. Danny tries to get us all to go back to his at the end of the night but I'm knackered and call it a night.

31

It's a Tuesday evening; I finished the station for the day a couple of hours ago and after tea went round to Liam's house.

So I'm sat in Liam's room, and it's a bit of a weird room, kind of like you'd imagine a fourteen-year-old boy's room would be like. It probably is. He still lives at home with his parents. But there's posters of football players on the wall; I'm pretty sure they are from English teams. They all seem to support English teams. I couldn't name the players but some of them have got to be about the same age as him. It might just be me, but isn't it a bit weird to worship people the same age as you?

I can understand looking up to people who are older and have done something but surely if you worship people your own age that's just highlighting how little you have managed to achieve, isn't it? And worshipping people younger than you is just wrong and freaky.

It worries me people my age and younger achieving stuff already; it's like I've been wasting my time all along.

We're at his place to chat about music and maybe how we could do something with him so as to maybe give him a shot at singing. It's a top-secret operation; he keeps saying, 'You won't tell no one, right?'

I'm not surprised he's so worried. For me, telling the lads about the radio thing was really hard; I'm not saying it was like coming out as a gaylord or anything, but anything that smacks of trying seems to be a real betrayal of the guy ethos. Like it's better to have not tried and not failed than to have tried and failed, and I'm not totally sure whether to try and succeed is better or worse than not trying and not succeeding.

I can see why Liam is scared to tell anyone. As a bloke, particularly the Johnny Big Bollocks that he's seen to be, people will rip the piss out of you if you try anything. Like the idea that I might possibly one day try to be a proper radio DJ. At least what I do at the moment is all right by them because (*a*) it's illegal; and (*b*) there's always the chance I might slip on some Warp 12-inch record to bend the grannies' minds.

Doh still thinks it's a bit fucked up that I'm friends with Liam, like we're not friends proper, we've just hung out a couple of times now. I'm scared though that someone – probably Fiona, knowing her – will blurt something out like: 'Oh Liam, you know Lex is obsessed with your girlfriend, right?'

Maybe this is like keep your friends close but your enemies closer? Except he's not really my enemy any more. I made him my enemy in my own head but he wasn't really; can you be an enemy if the person you are an enemy of doesn't agree to be your enemy? Like if a country is at war with another country does that other country automatically have to be at war with the other country back?

So we're searching through the Internet for auditions and ideas. We check *The Stage* website to see if there's anything online. It's mainly UK stuff but it's a start.

I don't know where to kick off really. I'm thinking if he was a success I could manage him, but he's never going to be a success, is he? I don't mean I'm humouring him doing all this, but I'm just saying odds-wise, it's unlikely isn't it? Still sometimes I let my imagination go a bit; if I was to manage him I'd need to smoke cigars and have a hand dripping in gold jewellery. I wonder if those managers of acts always looked like that and thus managing bands became a natural calling, or if they were like normal until they started managing a band and thought, this is the uniform I should be wearing. Like sergeants with their stripes: the more successful manager level you get to the more fat sovereign rings you add to your hand. The Svengali career progression.

We brainstorm. How lame is that? It takes us a while as Liam doesn't have any paper or pens in his room. I have loads of paper and notepads and pens; it's how I capture ideas. It's my net for trapping them, as if I don't get them down on some paper they could fly away and I'll never see them again. Not sounding too pretentious, but I don't think Liam has as many ideas as I do. If I go to London and the radio thing doesn't work out, I think I would be employable as I have a lot of ideas. People are always going to want people with ideas. How do you put that down on your CV?

Anyway we write down ideas: strengths/weaknesses, likes/dislikes, what he'd want to do, where, how to get better, who he would appeal to, what kind of act he'd like to be like.

It feels like we're actually getting somewhere when he says, 'Have a look at this,' and pulls up an image on his computer. It's of two women, naked, and they have both got a sort of Diet Coke bottle stuck in each other's bits.

Before I start on this bit of minor outrage I should clarify something. I'm a teenage guy, and reasonably adept on the computer, so obviously I've seen my fair share of porn, and obviously I abuse myself on a fairly regular basis. After all I'm a teenage boy and that is what I'm supposed to do, and it's not that I'm against porn; I mean it's naked women and what's not to like about that, but I find it's like the few times I've smoked hash: it just kind of numbs my brain for a period of time afterwards.

Davey likes to smoke hash sometimes and occasionally I've done it, but when I do, afterwards I always seem to get this feeling that my head is in this tight-fitting frame, like when someone has a neck injury and they get those head braces that latch onto their shoulders. And my brain has to be locked in until it's safe to go of its own accord.

Doh likes the wacky baccy too; I've kind of passed up on it enough times for them to know now that it's not really my thing so they don't really offer now if they're toking.

Don't get me wrong: I really would like to be good at taking drugs, just like I'd like to be good at walking, and I kind of think drugs would suit me and that I should have like a drug period in my life, but I just don't think I'm that good at taking them, so I tend to leave it. It just kind of feels like I'm letting my brain off the leash to run around like a greyhound loose in the park, and I worry it will run off into the woods and not come back, and I'm going to need my brain at some point. I think it's my main asset: well, it's better than the looks, the body and the personality, so by default it's the best asset.

It's the same with porn: when I look at it for any period of time, there's a while afterwards and it's like I'd been looking at a light bulb for too long and there's this glaze, like the image is burnt in and it's going to take a time for it to clear. So I'm like not that heavily into it: I kind of figure if you ration it a bit, when you do see some porn it's kind of a treat. Christ how uptight does that make me sound, a teenage lad who rations his porn intake, but I'm right, honestly, if you look at it all the time you end up looking at all the weird shit, like the weird shit that Liam is currently showing me.

I don't know if he's showing it to impress me or showing it to shock me. I don't know why he's showing it to me at all as we were trying to work on something here, and I thought we were getting somewhere, so he must be bored with that already; maybe he's got ADHD.

He then pulls up another naked picture on the computer. It loads slowly as he's got a shitey old PC. Gradually it comes on the screen, line by line and locking up occasionally. By halfway down the page I can see the picture, and it's of Michelle, and she's not wearing anything, and each extra line reveals a bit more of her, until eventually the full picture is showing.

It looks like the photo was taken in her bedroom. You can see her boobs, but she's got her hands clasped covering the pubic hair. He then starts showing me some more photos of her, each one taking its time to show on the screen. In one of them she's on the bed, and there's a couple where you actually see the lot, like full-on naked.

I felt awkward seeing it; on the way home I was thinking I should've stopped him, I should have stopped him straight away but I didn't. I did eventually, but I waited until he'd shown me about six or seven pictures before I said, 'You shouldn't be showing me things like that.' I mean what a hypocrite. I wait until I've seen enough of them before I take the moral high ground. Like, it was her, naked, which was great, but then I'm obviously betraying her just by looking at them. But still . . . it was her . . . naked.

When I told him to stop he was obviously embarrassed: I'd sort of told him off and he looked guilty about what he'd done.

I mean what kind of arsehole would do something like that to their girlfriend? I don't mean the taking the photos; maybe they both wanted to do it, but don't show it to your mates, that's fucking low. He's probably showed it to all his other friends too. Like I know I was out of order for looking but he was proper out of order for showing me in the first place.

And I can never understand girls who let guys do it anyway; they're idiots for doing it in the first place. I mean most couples split up, so there's a fair chance they are going to end up with the photos once you have split.

But what an arsehole. I had been starting to think he was a nice guy and that he was quite sensitive and shy, and then he goes and does that and shows really he's a total gimp.

After he did that I was thinking how long I would have to stay for before making my excuses to leave. I don't want him to know that that is the reason I want to get out of his house, but I don't want to stay in his room any longer than I have to now.

He offers me some solids, and that's when I make my more to leave. I tell him I've got work to do, then go get my bike and ride home.

On the way home I was thinking about what he'd just done and the thought came to me that actually he's just a kid, like he's got this big man's body but he was acting like a fucking kid in there. I mean he was just showing off, like showing me the porn and then offering me the drugs; he was trying to impress me. He's four years older than me and he's trying to impress me.

I suppose you could say it's like me when I bump into Andrew Farn. Andrew Farn is cool, he knows his music. He's away at UCD now but is the one person in this town who I think is cool. He's two years above me and is always into bands way before anyone else has heard of them.

Every time I see him for some reason I start spraying off music facts like a bleedin' machine gun, and all so he knows that I'm one of him, that I know my shit, that I'm cool. I always hate myself afterwards, but I suppose it's basically the same thing. I just want him to think I'm cool, to impress him and so he'll be my friend; of course he's far too fucking cool for that and I know it.

When I'm back home I start thinking about Liam's dream. I mean the simple and honest thing to do would be to tell him not to bother: there's only embarrassment and humiliation down the road he's going, with the smallest of small odds that it'll work for him, but you can't do that to someone's dream. You can't just put your arm around him and say, 'Listen it's best for all concerned if we never mention this again'; you've got to let them dream I suppose. I just wonder whether I am being cruel to him by egging him on.

But then I've got my dreams: maybe mine are as unrealistic as his; I just think they are do-able because they are my dreams and I somehow think it's going to work out for me.

Weird day over all but at the end of it I've seen Michelle naked, which is something.

Joke.

What is the difference between God and Bono?

God is the omnipotent supernatural creator and ruler of the universe and all within it.

Bono is a short-arsed eejit, who is the lead singer of a preposterously corny rock band, and everyone laughs at him behind his back.

32

DAVEY

Am well looking forward to this festival. I've got tons of tunes lined up to play in between all the acts; we're renting these total quality CD decks. There's gonna be plenty of girls there too, and like not from this town either. I'll be on the stage so I'll have a right good space to see which are the best-looking ones then go down and chat them up when the bands come on.

It's gonna be a proper good end of summer. The mum stuff was pretty rough. There's still the will stuff to do which hasn't been sorted yet, but got to keep going and that.

The kitchen has been so-so. It's been good to have something to distract me though; it's not as good in there as it was. Dravo has left; his visa had expired or something. I thought maybe I could step up to Sous but I've not really been doing it long enough: you need like six years to do that and I've not even done two. So they bought in this posh boy from Dublin called Eoghan. He's a total gobshite. Starts telling people they have to do it his way. He definitely wants Chef's job. Chef doesn't care as long as someone else is doing the work; he can just sit on his arse.

It's getting pretty soon until Lex goes. He seems pretty excited about it all. He's gonna have to toughen up in London otherwise people are just gonna take stuff off him. See that O'Shea tool. Seany tells me when I'm round there what he did with the ball and Lex has done nothing about it. That's just wrong. I may not get on that well with my family but for God's sake you've got to stick up for your little brother. I tried to tell him but he's always got some sort of excuse for not doing anything, some bullshit about it causing more trouble.

In the end I saw O'Shea in town and told him if he ever messes with Seany again I'm going to bite his face off.

O'Shea could probably do me, but he knows if he did try to do me I'm gonna hurt him too and that'll scare him enough not to mess any more.

You see that's Lex's problem, he's scared of getting hurt. He's more scared of it than how bad it actually is. Getting hurt doesn't hurt that much.

My brother used to batter me. You can get used to it, it's no biggie.

Maybe that should be my leaving present to him. I'll batter Lex for his own good. In the long run he'll thank me.

Still don't know what he's doing hanging round with that Liam horse, especially with his obsession with his girl. He's going to get a hoof in his mouth if he's not careful, that boy.

33

SATURDAY 26TH AUGUST

So the latest development from Chez Donal is this.

Since Ma and Dad went away for that weekend, they had a big old chat apparently; Ma said a lot of things that she's been keeping bottled up. Stuff about her having a bit of space, stuff about her not just being a housewife and mother, and stuff about wanting other interests, so it has come to this.

Fiona has gradually come to realise that she had really upset mum. Twenty years of marriage, eighteen years of me, eleven years of Fiona and eight years of Sean, and it was Fiona who finally broke Ma. And Ma was unbreakable: she was granite, emotionally and physically; she is the rock to which our family is grafted, until Fiona went and ballsed it up by breaking her with incessant, insensitive questioning. She's going to make an awesome trial lawyer.

Some poor defendant is going to end up screaming,

'I PLEAD GUILTY OK. JUST MAKE HER STOP WITH THE QUESTIONS.'

Ever since Ma's big blow-up in the kitchen it has been like eggshells when Fiona and Ma are in the same room. I know it was me she snapped at but it was because of Fiona she snapped and Fiona knows it.

Now, every Saturday we all have to go to Galway together: me, Da, Fiona and Sean, so we can leave Ma to have a bit of peace for the day. Some time to herself. 'She never gets any time to herself, and we owe it to her to give her some space.' So says Da, as we are driving out of town.

Sean is annoyed as he wanted to stay and play with his friend, and now he has to sit still in the car for an hour, which he finds impossible. He is in the back with Fiona. Fiona looks guilty; she has looked guilty for two weeks now. She knows she has done wrong and she has been trying to make it up to Ma and be extra nice to her. She even bought a top from a charity shop for her, but Ma isn't going to let her forget it that easy. She isn't ready to be friends again just yet and Fiona is feeling it. See for all her brains Ma still knows emotional power, and knows how to use it.

The car journey is slow. Da's put on some rubbish trad ceoil music; I ask him to turn it off but he's having none of it. I had begged him to be left at home too, as I had loads of stuff to do and I was going to be on the radio, but Da said no. He said we all had to go; he wasn't happy about it either but he knew that we had to go. We've done the journey to Galway a thousand times, and this has got to be one of the most painful. It's a Saturday in the summer, so it's a changeover day. The cottages get rented from Saturday to Saturday, so on Saturdays you get loads of people piling up from Dublin and stuff as well as all the people leaving to go back home, so it's pretty busy on the road.

No one is talking in the car; each has got their own gripe for why they are keeping quiet. I'm just thinking of all the shit I've got to get done for the festival. You see that's the problem with me and with music; if there's not music playing that I like or am listening to, then I'll start thinking, and when I start thinking that's when the problems occur.

Maybe the radio station, the whole love of music thing, is just one massive distraction to keep my head calm. I wonder if I could just sit in a room in silence for a day; I'd eat my own leg I reckon. That's got to be another reason to stay out of prison, other than the beatings and the arserape; just imagine me in solitary. If you wanted to torture me to get information out of me, don't bother pulling my nails out with pliers, just stick me in a room with my own brain for twenty minutes and leave me alone. Come back in later and I'll tell you fucking anything.

We park up in town. Da says to me to meet up at the car at 1.00 p.m., which gives us three hours to kill. Da has to take Sean and Fiona shopping. Fiona thinks she's old enough to be shopping on her own, and I'm sure Da would like to let her go too; it would save him having to be dragged round the shops for three hours by her, but he can't let her at this age. So Fiona is the one who behaved badly and the main person who is getting the punishment is Da. No wonder he was silent in the car on the way over.

I go to the Redlight and Zhivago record shops to pick up the money for the tickets they've sold and give them their fee from it which is €1 per ticket.

They sold out in all three shops and though I only gave them thirty for each, I'm still really happy about it, plus it's nice to chat to the guys about it and hang out in the shops. I don't get to talk much real muso stuff so I like it.

I skulk round the shelves for a bit too, to see if there's anything interesting in there. I'm going to get into the Rolling Stones; I've never really checked them out much. I buy *Exile on Main Street* for €13.

I sort of resent buying physical tunes these days; 95 per cent of my music is online and most of that was ripped for free, but I dig the shops and wanted to buy something and them see me buying something, plus it means I can walk round carrying a bag. If I have nothing to carry my arms like walk, y'know. Like if I'm carrying a bag it means my arms sway better when I walk, that's what I meant to say; when I'm not carrying anything they don't sway so well, and when I think about how they are swaying I like totally bollix up the natural swaying of them. I mentioned that shit walking bit earlier on; well the arm sway is all part of the rubbish walk thing.

I go get a coffee in a cafe and read *Uncut* magazine; I

bought it for a free Zeppelin CD on the cover. I've never dug Zeppelin; I know I should, I just don't. I'm going to try to listen to them some more, see if it works on me.

The rest of the time I mooch round a few of the shops. I see Da and Sean and Fiona a couple of times and pull back so they don't see me. Da is staring ahead ignoring Fiona who's talking and Sean who's hopping on one foot. If I were a decent son and not so selfish I'd join up with them and take them off Da's hands for a bit, but I'm not, which is something I should feel guiltier about than I do.

I meet them back at the car at 1.00 p.m. I'm stood by the car reading my magazine when they approach. Da looks at peace with them, relieved that he's done his shift.

On the drive back I put in the Zeppelin CD. Da lets two songs go before he turns it off and we have silence for all the rest of the trip.

I stare out of the window and think of all the things that need to be done for the festival when I get home; not long now. I've got a mental checklist to work through; there's a lot of admin and stuff that goes with the festival, making things go right. I know there are going to be some things that are going to go wrong on the day but I just hope it's nothing too major.

That evening I go to the Harp with Danny and Doh; we get our usual table. I get in about 9.00 p.m. as Ma made sure we all had tea together as a family and didn't eat our tea watching telly in the living room. This is another regime change: Saturday night we will have a family meal together and not in front of the telly.

I just wanted to get out. Ma tried to make conversation with Da; Da was shattered and didn't really want to talk; Fiona tried to make conversation with Ma but Ma was curt with her – I wonder to myself how long she can keep this up. Sean tried to make the smoothest mashed potato road in the world, and I watched the clock and tried to guess what the first acceptable time would be to ask if I could leave.

I felt really bad in the end though, as Da asked me if I wanted to go for a pint, and I said I was off to meet my buds. Then he said 'Can I come?' in this hopeful kind of voice, and I felt really bad; I mumbled some stuff and he knew I was sort of saying no, so he said not to worry about it but I felt a real shit, as he's had a rubbish day and probably just wanted a beer and some company to get out the house and the least I could've done was to have a pint with him and I turned him down.

I think he said something about giving Peter O'Reilly a shout, so hopefully he'll get out of the house.

In the pub Doh's girlfriend Stella was saying I should forget about Michelle and go out with her friend Amy, and that she would bring her out next time and I could meet her, but the thing is I know who she is already, although she's the year down, and she's all right and I think she's clever, but I'm just really not that bothered, you know.

At the pub Liam was leathered with his mates. I nodded

to him and he nodded back but he didn't come over and doesn't seem to when my friends are about, and I didn't go over to see him as his mates were being all like blokey and beery and that.

34

SUNDAY 27TH AUGUST – SIX DAYS TO THE CONCERT

So here I am, I'm finally on a date with Michelle. Liam is here too, but you can't have everything your own way. It's fucking weird man. It's Sunday night, bank holiday weekend, and we've driven to O'Dowds in Roundstone. My parents have taken us there before. The clam chowder dish there is unreal; I've had dreams about it before. It's like proper fish-mouth-food-warm-creamy-gorgeous.

It was supposed to just be Michelle and Liam together but he asked if I wanted to come along too; said it would be fine with Michelle; said we could talk to her about his singing idea and how it was all going to work. It appears I am now Liam's wingman.

It's a funny scene in the car. I'm sat in the back, and they don't seem to talk much: maybe it's because I'm there, maybe they just don't talk much in general. I'm sat behind Liam, who is driving. From where I am sat I can just see the shiny right side of Michelle's boob out the side of her top, and she's not wearing a bra. Her boob bounces when the car goes over bumps and drains. And just so we're all clear about this, I may be the hero of this story and you may be looking down on me right now for being a little pervert, but let's just remember that I'm still a teenage boy and a good boob is still a good boob, and it bounces every time we go over a bump, so I'm going to watch it all the way along the R341 to Roundstone.

The restaurant looks out over the bay. It's just starting to get cold in the evening, and the harbour waters are still as that part of the ocean settles down for the night.

Liam parks up and gives Michelle the keys, as she'll be driving back. We walk down the hill and Michelle walks ahead. 'Everything OK?' I ask Liam.

'Ahh, she just gets in these strops sometimes, I don't know why; she's just a bleedin' pain in the arse now and again, y'know?'

We continue walking down, and we are ten yards from the restaurant and Michelle is holding the door open when Liam flicks my arm with the back of his hand and says, 'Let's not talk about the singing tonight, hey? Not the right time, y'know.'

Our secret mission continues.

I nod in understanding, and head on in.

Liam goes to the bar to get the drinks, and Michelle and I go and get our table, and I'm sat there, opposite her, opposite *the* Michelle O'Reilly, *the* stunning Michelle O'Reilly. Like after all this time I'm finally sat directly opposite her, and not over a deli counter, and not staring at her from afar but opposite her, touching distance, me and her.

She starts talking to me; she seems all happy talking to me, maybe the mood she was in is just exclusively for Liam.

'So you not got a girl of your own, Mister Lex? A guy like you should have his own girl, you shouldn't have to be spending your Sunday nights with a dull old couple like us.'

'Ah y'know, I had nothing on like, and Liam was insistent and all.'

'Yeah, Liam can be insistent,' she says in a sigh.

I shrug, and twist my lips.

'You're a good-looking boy you know, Mister Lex, you could do well with the ladies. I bet you could have your pick of the girls in your year.'

I'm a bit embarrassed at this. I think: it's not the girls in my year I'm interested in, it's the girl in the year above. The one sat opposite me, the one with a mouth and a smile and eyes and boobs and who's just bloody gorgeous and who's just sat there in front of me.

'Not really,' I say.

'Sure it is, I could set you up with some people if you'd like?'

It's all a bit awkward. I think of saying, well set me up with you, but of course I don't do it, as I'm always too chicken-shit to do it.

You could fill a lifetime with things that I've been too chicken-shit to do, or will be too chicken-shit to do. I need to accept that I am the sort of person who is too chicken-shit to do stuff, so I'm never going to do it anyway, so if I was never going to do it anyway that means I wasn't too chicken-shit to do it, because I was never going to do it.

My logic circle breaks down when I realise later that having an idea and wanting to do the idea and then not doing it means that actually I am too chicken-shit. I should keep a tally for my life or maybe just for a year: have one year when I tally up all the things I was too chicken-shit to do and another where I did the things I might have been too chicken-shit to do, and then at the end of the two years work out which route is best for me. I fear the one that is probably the best for me is the not being chicken-shit, which is why I probably won't do it, as I'm too chicken-shit to find out, thus proving my point.

Like the festival and the radio station, they are ideas I had, good ideas, and I followed them through and they've been a success, well, the radio station has been and the festival hopefully will be, so I should learn from that, I should learn to just take a chance and things can work out for the best.

Back to O'Dowd's. The main thought in my head is, 'I've seen a photo of you naked, I've seen a photo of you naked, I've seen a photo of you naked, I'VE SEEN A PHOTO OF YOU NAKED.' It's amazing: I was delighted in the back of the car to just see a quarter of her boob, when I have already seen the whole of her naked, muff and everything.

I try to come up with some conversation which is not about me and girls but all my mind is saying is, I've seen a photo of you naked, and I know what your bush looks like.

I wonder if she can see it in my eyes, I wonder if she suspects that Liam might show photos of her to other people.

In the end I blurt out some rubbish about Liam being deadly at football, figuring Liam's something we have in common we could talk about, but Michelle decides to take it as a cue to start slagging him off, saying he's boring and that he bullies her. It makes me feel uncomfortable. I should be revelling in it, I should put the boot in to him but I don't.

Maybe Liam is a tactical genius; maybe by making me his friend he has managed to neuter my threat with Michelle (if there ever was a threat, which I'm starting to believe is highly unlikely). Or maybe he's let the Trojan horse into the castle, and from there I can attack. Or maybe, and this is far more likely, I'm some sort of Trojan Shetland pony, who's been invited in only to realise I'm no threat at all.

I'm not really a threat now, though; I'm not the sort to exploit someone's kindness, really. If someone is nice to me I am extremely weak at the selfish bit and not honouring that niceness back, even if it was to get a crack at Michelle.

Eventually Liam comes over with two pints for me and him and a Diet Coke for Michelle.

Michelle goes from being animated to quiet again.

The conversation ends up being like a triangle with only

two sides. Liam talks to me, I talk to Liam; Michelle talks to me, I talk to Michelle; Liam and Michelle rarely talk to each other, like we will all three be in the same conversation but it all goes through me. In the end I end up talking about myself an awful lot: about my plans, about the festival, about the radio station and about London.

Both Michelle and Liam seem excited about the festival. Liam's bought a Toots and the Maytals CD (see, my work with the radio station is paying off, influencing people's music choices) to learn all their songs. Michelle is going with a big group of her girly friends. Bearing in mind that they are both going to go, probably together, it's a bit weird that they don't talk about their plans.

It's six days to go until the festival; I am trying to just calm myself down about it all. Almost everything has been arranged now: catering stalls, beer licence, hotels booked, deposit on giant tent, deposit on the sound desk, lights, rigging and equipment, all bands confirmed, timings finalised, temporary toilets booked. That we've sold out the whole thing is brilliant: I even have people asking if they can get any more tickets. I think about printing up a few more this week and selling them; these tickets are pure profit and no one is going to notice if there are fifty more people in there. It's not like the fire brigade are going to turn up and count everyone.

Sometimes, just sometimes, I think I really might just pull off this festival and become Lex Donal – concert promoter.

After talking myself out about the festival, I talk about

my plans for college. Maybe this being a narcissist means I'll never be stuck for something to talk about. It saves the evening here though. When Liam gets up to go to the toilet, Michelle starts to slag him off again.

When Michelle goes to the toilet Liam starts at me, asking what her problem is.

When I go to the loo and come back they are both sat in silence looking straight ahead. Fortunately I am getting a little drunker now so I am less sensitive to the awkwardness of it all.

In the car on the way back I'm just babbling away. Michelle now looks fucked off with the pair of us, which is easy to understand when she's sober and we're as pissed as farts. There's nothing more annoying, even before taking into account being already pissed off with your boyfriend.

I sit on the opposite side of the back seat on the way back and I struggle to concentrate on her quarter-boob on the way home, but keep talking rubbish and getting distracted.

Michelle drops me off at my house and makes a big show of saying how much she enjoyed herself. She gives me a kiss on the cheek as she lets me out of the car on her side, even though Liam was moving to let me out and it was easier to get out his side.

Girls are mental.

The car drives off and I know they are headed for a right barney. I wonder if Liam can keep his mouth shut until he gets home.

I go upstairs, put my headphones on, turn the light off

and listen to some David Bowie. I decided to listen to it lying on the floor with my eyes closed and hands clasped across my chest coffin-style, as I think this will make it sound better.

I drift off to sleep trying to work out if the siren I can hear is on the CD or is coming from somewhere in town.

35

MONDAY 28TH AUGUST – FIVE DAYS TO THE CONCERT

Fuck
Fuck
Fuck
Fucking Celtic tiger
Fucking teachers
Fucking cookery shows
Fucking Celtic tiger cookery shows
Fucking pretentious foodie wankers
Fucking middle-class foodie Celtic tiger wankers
Fucking snobby wanky foodie Celtic tiger wankers
Fucking teachers
Fucking chefs
Fucking science teachers
Fucking waiters
Fucking steak
Fucking gastro-wank-off steak wanky foodie wankers

But at the end of the day and most of all, fucking Davey Mahon.

You total piece of shit.

36

FIONA

Lex has been crying in his room. He's been crying all morning; no one will tell me why he's been crying. I think Mum and Dad know. I don't think anyone has died; we would have been told if someone had died. It's not the exams; he passed those, unless they called to say they were wrong and there's been a mistake.

He comes out of his room to use the phone and takes it into his room and shouts into it, then he puts the phone back outside the room.

It's really sad to hear him cry. I want to tell him it will be all right and not to be so sad but Mum tells me I'm not allowed to go up there and says that Sean and I have to go to the shops to get her some orange juice, but I know we have already got at least half a carton of orange juice.

I think Mummy is going to go in and talk to him when we go out. Mummy and Daddy are both in the kitchen talking about what they should do. Sean and I heard them from the corridor.

Daddy looks scared and he doesn't want to go in to talk to him; he thinks they should just leave him to calm down and go up later. He could be trying to get Mum to go and talk to Lex. Women are better at talking than boys.

37

MA

I took the phone call. It was from Mr Maguire, the headmaster of the school. He called at 9.00 a.m. I vaguely remembered hearing the sirens going last night and thought it was strange that there were so many; apparently some had come all the way from Galway.

He said there had been a fire at the school and that David Mahon was the main suspect for it and that he had been arrested just outside the grounds of the school last night.

He had been seen by someone whose house backs onto the grounds, after they had been woken by the sound of breaking glass. They've had a few break-ins at the school before. They watched him leave across the school grounds and climb the fence and then they saw the flames from the science wing.

Mr Maguire said given the severity of the crime and because David and Lex are linked and such close friends it would be unwise for them to let Lex's concert go ahead. He said it would be extremely inappropriate for the best friend of the person who set fire to the school to be allowed to host an event at the school less than a week after it had happened.

I tried to persuade him otherwise. I told him how far the arrangements had gone and that David has had a really tough time with his mother dying. And I said they shouldn't punish my boy because of another boy's mistake. He said he understood; he said that he'd not known about David's mother dying, but that it was still no excuse for what he did. He said he had spoken to two of the governors and they had both agreed. He said it was an unfortunate circumstance but that the decision had to be taken and it had. He also added that maybe the decision would make David consider his actions more.

The sad thing is David was always going to do something silly to get himself into trouble. As a parent you can see who things like this will happen to and who it won't. At some point in the future he was always going to go too far and this is it. I warned Lex about him before, but the more you warned him, the more he stuck up for his friend. I tried the other approach, to be extra nice to David and invite him over in the hope it would work the opposite way, but that didn't help either.

But a mother knows a threat to their offspring when they see one, even when it comes as a friend. Especially as it comes as a friend, because then the child can't see the danger themselves.

If you play with fireworks eventually one's going to go off in your face.

At least no one got hurt. Apparently it is only one classroom that has been damaged but it is still a very serious crime; they could send him to prison for this.

So it was up to me to tell Lex. He was still asleep when the call had come. Some mornings he stays in bed too long, sets the radio station going, turns the volume down and goes back to bed. I've told him that I don't think he is setting a good example doing this, that he should be there at regular times as people get used to it and expect him at certain times of the day. It is confusing for listeners when there isn't a structure.

If he is going to do this radio thing professionally one day, he won't be able to decide that he just can't be bothered some days. He needs to set himself the discipline and not to have to have it set for him.

So I left him to sleep until 10.00 a.m. He had been out with Michelle and her boyfriend last night and came back a bit drunk.

I went up there with a cup of tea. I felt truly awful having to tell him; it just broke his heart.

He started talking about other places he could move it to.

His face, once he'd realised what I'd said, just locked. He kept saying, 'But why?' 'How do they know?' and 'But why?' over and over again.

I left him for a few hours: he's got a lot of things to think about. I told him I thought he should call Mr Maguire and talk to him about it, to see if there was any chance of saving the situation.

Poor boy, he doesn't deserve this after all the hard work he has put into the festival thing. It's rotten luck.

38

Fucking Davey Mahon.

Fucking Davey Mahon, he's fucked the whole thing up, the whole bloody show: the festival, Toots and the Maytals coming over in five days time, *the* Toots and the Maytals coming over to Clifden, to play in Clifden, for me and the town, and he's fucked the fucking lot of it.

The festival has been cancelled. The school called up and said that we can't put the show on there any more. I didn't think to have a contract with them or anything like that; it was just an agreement between me and Mr Maguire that we could put the show on the playing fields, and now we can't because of that cocksucker Davey Mahon.

You see Davey managed to have the foresight and wisdom to set fire to one of the classrooms at the school and now because Davey is my best friend, I am not allowed to put on the show, and now I have to phone Toots and the Maytals to say it's cancelled, call the tent people, call the sound people, call the food people, not to mention refund everyone for their bloody tickets, and it's Davey's fault, all because of a piece of fucking steak.

Peter O'Reilly let Ma know what had happened. She called him at the station after Mr Maguire called the house, so she could find out from him what had happened.

Davey is still in the cells down there; they've not let him go as there's no one to pick him up, him not being eighteen yet. With his mum gone, they've been unable to get hold of his brothers. My ma would go but she's obviously angry with him too, so he's just sat there at the moment.

He has admitted it all. He told them when he sobered up this morning, and Peter O'Reilly has since told Ma.

So apparently what happened was the normal head chef at the hotel wasn't there last night, so one of the other guys took over as head chef. And Davey was doing the meat bit, and Mr Sherbourne who is a teacher at our school comes in with his wife for dinner.

Davey sees it's him, and when the order comes in for his table, it's a steak for him, and it's medium rare.

Mr Sherbourne along with a lot of the teachers at school always thought Davey was an eejit, so Davey thinks, I'm going to do this steak and I'm going to do it good, and when Mr Sherbourne enjoys it, I'm going to bump into him at the end of the meal as he leaves and ask him how he liked his steak and when he says he liked it, I'll tell him I cooked it and I'm not such a fuck-up after all; this is Davey's big plan.

So Davey takes out the best-looking steak that has been

prepped and fires it. Two minutes each side then leaves it to rest.

The call comes and it gets sent out, with the fish for his wife. Two minutes later the steak comes back: it's rare, it's too bloody, he wanted medium rare. 'You do know what medium rare is?' says the chef. 'Stick it on for another two minutes.'

The stand-in head chef guy gives him more of a bollocking and he sticks it back on, then he sends it out again.

And this time it comes back again; this time he's complaining that it's too well done now, and that it's still not what he ordered. He'd said he'd eat it but he's not paying for it, but the waiter says no, we'll cook it again, we'll get it right and we'll do your wife's main course again too. He apologises and goes back to the kitchen.

So the waiter comes back to the kitchen and shouts at the stand-in head chef, and the stand-in head chef shouts at Davey, and Davey is boiling up, but he cooks another steak. Halfway through the cooking, the stand-in head chef kicks Davey off the grill and makes him go out the back and prep vegetables.

Davey is really angry, and at the end of the meal the waiter asks if Mr Sherbourne would like to see the chef as the chef wishes to apologise. Mr Sherbourne comes back and he apologises for sending back the steak, but says it was a special meal for him and his wife. The stand-in head chef apologises for the steak and says he had every right to send it back.

Davey comes out the back after finishing his work and

the stand-in head chef tells Mr Sherbourne who the guilty party was, which is pretty shitty like, as he's the chef so it should be down to him not to serve it in the first place. So anyway Mr Sherbourne sees it was Davey Mahon, as Davey looks up and Sherbourne shakes his head at Davey, like as if Davey's not gutted as it is.

So Davey probably imagines what Mr Sherbourne is thinking and his humiliation is total, and that is when the switch has gone.

And then after service Davey is sat out the back steps of the kitchen, waiting for the stand-in head chef to come out, and when he did Davey tries to fight him. After that, he snuck into the bar area, stole some beers, stole a steak and a plate, then went up to the school, broke in through a skylight and set fire to a desk in Mr Sherbourne's science class, the table having the steak on a plate on top of it.

And that is why there is no festival, because Davey is a fucking idiot and he can't cook a steak, and it hurts every time I think about it.

There is no festival.

A day later and he hasn't even phoned. I don't want to speak to him but he could've called, or he could've got word to me that he was sorry.

He hasn't told Danny or Doh that's he's sorry either. If he'd have done that then they could've told me and at least I'd then know he regretted what he did, and know he knows how much he's fucked things up for me.

39

I spent the rest of day in a daze. It's Monday, I don't know if to call and cancel today; I don't know if there's any way of saving it. It's a bank holiday so the tent and music people probably won't be contactable.

I try to think of other places to stage it but there's nowhere really big enough. A football pitch isn't big enough; the school had the biggest field around, and nowhere else is flat enough.

I should call the tour manager of Toots, but I can't bear to at the moment.

Michelle has asked to meet up with me. I should be more excited but I'm too depressed.

She asked me to meet her at the play area over by Waterfall Homes; she sent a text to the radio mobile number. 'Can you meet me tonight at the swings behind the field?' it said. 'I really need to talk to you.'

It seemed very secretive so it must be something good. I spent ages going over what '*really*' and '*need*' meant. Why would she '*really*' '*need*' to speak to me?

I always over-think everything, it's one of my things, and even after over-thinking, the conclusion I get to is almost always wrong anyway. So when she asked to meet me I thought of all the possible reasons she wanted to see me, knowing that everything I thought of would be the wrong answer, leaving one option as the right answer. So if I could just manage to think of every single possible reason why she might want to see me other than that she wanted to show me her tits, it would leave the only option left being that she wanted to show me her tits, so it could logically only be that outcome.

The reasons I had so far:

She wants to talk about Liam – bad. She's annoyed with him.
She wants to talk about Liam – good. She wants to do something special for him.
She wants to go back to school.
She wants to move to London.
She wants to dump Liam.
She wants to talk about Liam, to dump him, to go with me to London and to go to school there and to show me her tits as a prelude to what I would be seeing a lot more of once I was in London.

It's hard to stay off the tits thought process knowing you are trying to stay off the tits thought process. It's like 'Don't touch the button.'

She said meet at 9.30 p.m.; it was dark by then. I got

there fifteen minutes early. Danny and Doh had texted saying they were going to the Harp tonight but I didn't fancy it. I'm trying to stay out of public view since the festival thing went to shite.

I haven't officially announced it's off yet, though some people know as something like that flies round town. I just feel people staring at me like I've got some sort of facial wart; it's probably just my guilt.

People love to watch a massive failure, and I am that massive failure whether they know it yet or not.

I couldn't handle someone coming up to me and saying something about it all, or me having to explain what happened.

On the way over I saw that Patrick O'Shea and his little team of rat boys. If he'd've known it was cancelled he'd've given us a right slagging. Even if he didn't know it was cancelled he would have given us a slagging. Strangely this time he did nothing; I just walked past him and he didn't say anything. And it's not like he didn't see me; he saw me and just chose not to do anything. Maybe that's one of the benefits of being mates with Liam.

Back to the meet with Michelle.

So I got there fifteen minutes before she had said. I'm always early; it is an annoying habit but I just am. I sit there on the swings waiting, pushing myself with my foot on the back swing. I'm going over again what I think it is she wants to talk about. I think it could well be Liam has told her and she doesn't want him to do the singing thing. I could imagine she wouldn't want him to humiliate himself; maybe she just wants to protect him and thinks he'll actually listen to me, or maybe it will embarrass her.

Maybe it's some other issue with Liam, as since we've become friends, and I'd say we probably are now, he probably talks to me more about the sort of stuff Michelle would want to talk about than his buds would.

While I'm waiting I start to think about Michelle and what she wants; like when I think of Michelle I always think what I want, but I never think what she wants. I've never stopped to think what she might be hoping for; maybe if I understood that more I would understand her more, and maybe then I'd stand a better chance with her.

Like I don't even know what she wants in life. She's nineteen and the prettiest girl in our town; that's got to be kind of hard for her in a way, and like girls with the burden of their looks, like: it's obvious she's pretty, but then if she knows she's pretty then everyone is going to think she's a stuck-up bitch, but like if she didn't know it it's pretty disingenuous y'know. Either way like girls are going to hate her cos they always hate pretty girls don't they.

Eventually she turns up.

'Hey, you,' she says and flashes me her teeth.

'Thank you sooo much for coming out,' she says, dragging out the 'so' like it's a note, '. . . and like sorry for all the hush-hush.' She says, 'I just wanted someone to talk to who was a bit smart and that I know I could talk to and that wouldn't tell anyone else, because you wouldn't would you?'

'Of course not,' I says. '. . . Is everything OK?'

'Ahh yes and no, I don't know; I just wanted someone to talk to, you know, someone separate like. I can't talk to my girlfriends; they all think Liam is great.'

I don't tell her that I'm pretty sure they think he's a dick actually.

'I suppose so. I dunno. Yes, no, I dunno; I just don't know what I'm doing I suppose? Do you know what I mean? Like, I'm just so confused. Y'know, I can't stay behind the counter at the Super-Value all my life, and Liam, God bless him, I love Liam, but sometimes I just don't know where it's going; sometimes I think I should just split and leave this town. If I split with Liam I couldn't stay here; I'd see him all the time and stuff, and he'd get another girl like *that*, and I'd probably know her and it'd be all awkward . . .'

Suddenly I'm the town counsellor: first Liam's dreams, now Michelle's fears, and I don't know what to say. Two weeks ago I'd've told her to dump the ballsack, but that was two weeks ago, and now I've found out he's not that bad when you get to know him, although sometimes he is. Besides, she's not saying dump him for me is she, there's no hint of me in the afterthought. It's a talk about her, not a talk about us; it's a talk about him.

So that would mean neither of us would have her and I'd then have to find whatever new guy she went out with and start to fixate over him.

If I told her to dump him it would be pretty low of me. I mean I do still like her; maybe I'm a bit less obsessed with her than before now I know her a little, but she's still a delight to look at.

I trot out some rubbish about her already knowing inside what the right answer is, sort of hinting that she should dump him without actually saying so, telling her to be brave and you only live once, which is all but saying, 'Listen girl, if you really want to do it, do it and stop wasting my time.'

I sound like one of Fiona's magazines. I know this as I have read a few of them, purely for research purposes though, obviously, to understand women in general: not that it's done me much good.

I think of trying to pitch the 'What about me?' angle, but I've started to realise I'm not really a contender. I'm a sweet puppy, a thing that's nice to have around, but I'm not going to do anything but embarrass myself if I make a play for her now. I mean I think this, I'm like 98 per cent certain; there's still 2 per cent of me that thinks just go for it: just give her a kiss or something, at least let her know how you feel, but I don't.

'Thanks for the talk, Lex,' she says. 'You're a good guy, so y'are. Some girl is going to get real lucky one day,' and she kisses me goodbye, but it's a kiss on the side of the lips, like just where the side of my mouth becomes the cheek, like maybe it was cheek and she missed slightly. Or maybe she was going for mouth a bit not the cheek, like why would you go for that bit, what's she trying to say by doing that? Like if you're going to kiss them on the cheek you kiss them on the cheek; if you're going to kiss them on the mouth you kiss them on the mouth. What's this side-of-the-mouth thing, what did it mean?

Regardless, a little bit of blood rushes right down there straight away.

She walks off and her arse wiggles perfectly in the tight jeans. I remember again why everyone fancies her.

Oh in case you were wondering, she didn't show me her tits, but then I would have told you that, wouldn't I?

40

MA

I don't want Lex to go. I can finally say it to myself, I can finally say it to my friends. I can't say it to Lex's father; it's not something he wants to hear, but I don't want him to go. He's my boy, my angel. I have to let him go; you raise them to let them go; I wouldn't want him to stay here all his life, it would be such a waste, but I want him to stay here all his life: I want him to stay with me.

The first time I ever saw him, the first time I ever held him, after twenty-one hours of labour and pain I couldn't have known, I could see how special he was; his eyes. He still looks like that little ball when he came out; I can still see that baby in him.

There was no Michael with me; you didn't have the men in with you in those days, just a dragon of a midwife who'd seen it all before. The relief when he came out just so I wouldn't have to see that terrible woman again. I see Lex and I think of the happiness I felt when I first saw him; I think of the midwife and I just think of the pain.

But Lex is special. I want him to go and show the world, but I want him to be back home for tea.

I thought of going over myself and staying with him. He'd hate that; I'd embarrass him, like when I was going to become a dinner lady at the school he did everything he could to persuade me not to. He doesn't want me to see the other side, the side with his friends. I can see it though.

When he goes I know it's going to take me a while to get over it: it'll be like a bereavement. It's not like he's going to be gone for good; he'll still come back and we'll go over, but it just feels like an end. He doesn't know it but I like to think of him as my friend sometimes. He'd hate to think I was his friend but I am. I love it when we chat too; the only time these days he will chat is if he's had a drink with his pals, then when he comes home he lets his guard down and treats me as if I'm not his mum.

I'd love to go out with him and his friends and see what he's like around them. I bet he's funny with them, relaxed and natural.

I still hope he'll come back and settle in Ireland, maybe go to England, learn some things and then come back here and use it. Clifden may be too small for him, but Galway or Dublin could be just right. I can't see us moving but I'm not against it, not once the other two are grown up.

I suppose it's a warning about the new chapter that's going

to come round once Fiona and Sean come of age. Fiona is definitely going to fly the nest; Sean may take a bit longer to shift, though he could surprise us all.

But once they are gone it'll just be me and Michael and Clifden. We've got friends, lots of friends, but things could get boring.

The photography course I've started I am really enjoying. I've got a brand new super-duper camera that I can get photos up on the computer. It's so long since I've learned stuff. It's nice to keep Fiona quiet once in a while too; it's good for her to know that her parents have feelings too.

She got really scared when I flipped out, and I scared myself too; I didn't realise how angry and worried I was. But it's for the best: I'm doing something now and hopefully if I can achieve a pass who knows where it could lead, and the break they give me on a Saturday is just bliss.

I needed something to kick me like that though: I've just been a mum for so long now I'd forgotten there was more to me than that. It wasn't all I wanted when growing up, though it is what I mainly wanted, a good husband and a good family.

I was never as driven as Fiona, I was never as clever, but I have to say I don't think I was as annoying either. She may have to watch that as she grows.

But Lex, Lex is going to break my heart.

41

TUESDAY 29TH AUGUST

There's so much shit happening with the fallout of the festival not happening now, I finally bit the bullet and called the people up to say it was off.

The money side is the biggest problem.

It was supposed to work like this:

Original Costs	
Toots	€15,000.00 [Usual fee €25k $30,000]
Tent	€5,000.00
Sound	€4,000.00
Lights	€4,000.00
Electricity	€1,000.00
Band 2	€700.00
Band 3	€200.00
Band 4	€200.00

Hotel	€800.00
Insurance	€979.00
Prep stuff	€500.00
Selling fee	€1,600.00 [€1 per ticket]
Posters	€500.00 printing [did design myself]
Tickets	€100.00 printing
Portaloos	€1,000.00
	€35,579.00
Income	€36,400
	€821.00 profit

Instead it's come out like this:

Cancellation costs

Toots	[No deposit]
Tent	€1,500.00 [Deposit]
Sound	€1,000.00 [Deposit]
Lights	€1,000.00 [Deposit]
Electricity	
Band 2	
Band 3	
Band 4	
Hotel	
Insurance	€979.00 [Paid up-front]
Prep stuff	

Selling fee	€1,600.00
Posters	
Tickets	
Portaloos	€250.00

€6,329.00 total cost to me

€6,531.00 savings in bank before Davey Mahon ruined my fucking life

€202.00 savings in bank after

The manager of Toots and the Maytals went nuts, says he's going to sue me for cancelling the gig. I didn't have to pay any money up front to them in return for paying them cash on the day. So they are left with nothing.

The tent and the stage and the sound and light people are a different matter. They've already got €3,500 deposit; I'm not going to see that again. They say there is a cancellation charge of €6,000: I don't have that; I've told them I don't have it. They've phoned up a couple of times and have been aggressive. They've left messages on the phone. I've told Ma if they phone the house just say I don't live there any more.

It's more bloody grief dealing with the fallout of it all than if the thing had gone ahead.

I had to go into Galway to tell the two record shops that it had been cancelled and give them the money back to refund to the people who bought the tickets from there.

And obviously I didn't get their commission back so that's going to cost me.

I announced it was cancelled on the station and I had to print up banners to put over the posters saying it has been cancelled.

In short the whole thing is going to cost me €6,329. It's the last time I'm going to try anything ever again.

42

Clifden doesn't have a Starbucks. In Starbucks' desire to dominate the world coffee market, not even they can be bothered with the town of Clifden; it's another sign I have to get away. I think it would do well here; people would go there to meet instead of going to the pub. Our livers would be better but we'd be a bit more wired.

Michelle has texted me to ask if she can meet me again. This time I know it's to talk about Liam, as it said so in her text.

I suggest we meet at the Corner Café and have a coffee there. It's not a pub, and it means we won't have to stay too long. I feel a bit weird like meeting her in public; like she's not my girl, so I shouldn't really be seen hanging around with her too much if Liam isn't about.

The first time it was at night and by the swings so no one saw us. This time it's like, what if someone says something to someone who says something to Liam, like, 'I saw your missus out with that wee fecker Lex yesterday': that's going to annoy him, isn't it, like I wouldn't expect Doh to meet up with my missus if I ever had one, not unless they were like proper mates beforehand which me and Michelle weren't. I mean, I knew her and bought sandwiches off her but I wasn't like a mate or anything.

I thought about phoning Liam up and saying, look your missus wanted to meet up for a coffee, is that cool like? I wonder if he has any idea that I still really dig his girl. I mean I'm a bit less obsessed now I know them y'know, but like I definitely would, I really would. Like the collapse of the festival, it's something that I'm trying to stop thinking about.

She's already there when I get to the café. I get a straight coffee. They don't do cappuccinos or lattes: that the cup is clean and the drink is hot is good enough.

I sit down opposite her on the fixed orange plastic chair.

She starts talking the moment I am in the seat.

'Liam asked me to marry him,' she says. 'I'm like nineteen, I don't want to get married yet. Like, I don't want another boyfriend or anything, I just think it's a bit young for me to be marrying someone. I want to be at least twenty-three.'

So from possibly dumping him, to now maybe marrying him, in a week. It's a big turnaround, though I think she'll say no.

'What did you say to him?' I ask.

'I said I didn't know, that I'd think about it, that we were a bit young, that it wasn't a no.'

'Tell him it's a "not yet",' I suggest. 'That way it's not a straight no, but it's not a yes either.'

'But what if he gets angry; he scares me when he gets angry.'

I say, you can't just marry a guy because you're scared of him, in fact that's the worst reason; in fact if you're scared of him you shouldn't even be with him.

'What am I going to do, Lex? I can't tell the girls; they all want me to marry him so they can be bridesmaids.'

I'm sure she's wrong on this: as I said before I'm pretty sure they think he's a dick. Maybe they are just being nice to her face; maybe they are too scared to tell her what they really think.

She scrapes the edge of her hot chocolate, and uses her finger to get up bits of powdered chocolate.

I'm less in awe of her recently; I suppose that's exposure. I mean my heart started going really quickly when I walked in, but it's not as bad as before, no bright-red face any more.

I honestly don't know what to say to her now though; she's speaking to me and not her friends about it because maybe she wants a different opinion from the one they are going to give her. It's weird that out of all the people she could have chosen she chose me. I suppose it's another sign that I am a friend, and friend material, but not boyfriend/lover material. I suppose it's better than nothing, though being this close could be even worse and still makes me think what if.

I still think I might try to kiss her before I leave town. Just to have kissed her, just to have tried, to have soared only to burn, to have soared for that one second before she pulled away would be epic: imagine if I had to leave town just for one second of a kiss. If she pulled away before I even got my lips on hers that would be too awful, knowing I tried and failed and was humiliated (that being said, I am getting used to humiliation); not to try and fail but in between trying and failing to have one second of success. Did I ever mention her lips, oh man they look so soft, like shiny marshmallows, oh man touching them with my lips would just be the connection to another world.

She's still talking. I decide to stop her.

'OK, here's what I think. You need to think about this logically, like a bloke – do you want to spend the rest of your life with him?'

'No,' she says fairly clearly.

'Do you want to spend the next year with him?'

'Yes, errr no, I don't know: that's what the problem is.'

'I can't help you Michelle, I'm sorry, all I can do is tell you to do what feels right.'

'But I don't know what feels right.'

I'm getting frustrated by her now.

'Fuck it then, dump him and if it feels wrong after go back out with him; that way you will have tried both routes.'

'But what if after I dump him he goes off with someone else? All the girls like him, you know that.' It's a phrase I've heard many times before, like this slightly slow, admittedly physically quite impressive person is the perfect specimen for the eligible female to aspire to in our town. It's probably for the best I leave this town. At least in London although there might be more Alpha Males I'm hoping there will also be a reasonable portion of women who don't look at a Liam Dansey like he's some sort of gift from the Man.

'Oh shit,' says Michelle suddenly.

'What?'

'That was Liam's sister Teresa, she just walked past,' she says looking out.

'I should really go,' she says; she seemed really shook up by the girl seeing her.

And with that she gets up and leaves.

43

FIONA

An American man phoned up to speak to Lex. He called twice in an hour. The second time he asked if I worked at Radio Clifden and what I did there. I told him that yes I did work there and I was Lex's executive assistant and if he had anything to say to Lex he should say it to me.

He shouted at me to make Lex phone him. I told him he was not allowed to shout at me.

I told him Lex would not speak to anyone who was rude.

He shouted some more.

When he calmed down he said unless he heard from Lex by the end of the day that he would start legal 'pro-seeding' against Radio Clifden and that he would shut the station down.

I told him the station was shutting down anyway because Lex had to go away.

He asked me where Lex was going and I said Moscow to join the Bolshoi. I want to join the Bolshoi one day, but it is very hard. They are the best dancers in the world. I need to make sure I don't grow too much.

I know I shouldn't lie but he sounded like a bad man.

44

WEDNESDAY 30TH AUGUST

This cancelled festival has caused me huge embarrassment in what was until two days ago my hometown. It is now the town I grew up in, it isn't my hometown any more and I can't wait to get out of here. It has changed, and I've changed. I'm embarrassed walking down the streets; I don't want to go to the Harp as I know the ear-bending I'm going to get.

Not only has Davey cost me this embarrassment in my hometown, he's also cost me, financially, a lot.

So the €6,531 I had in my account, this was my money saved up from the computer jobs and such; it has taken me about three years to get together. I spent little bits on equipment but almost all the money I earned I saved, so that when I get to London I can actually go out and do the things and see the things and not have to get a job or live on the breadline. I don't need much in the way of food and comfort but I'm going out to see as many bands as possible. I was going to be a kid in a sweetshop: so much to see, so much to do, and with a bit of money I would actually be able to do it. Apparently the first year's work at college is not that hard, so I wouldn't need to knuckle down too much.

Anyway thanks to Davey that €6,531 is looking like being down to €202; basically that fucker's little stunt has cost me the best part of six and a half grand.

I priced the whole show up so that I would have about €1,000 profit: I knew there would have been a few costs that I would have forgotten like the insurance and the posters, so that was my leeway for when things went wrong.

I used a fair chunk of the money I had in the bank to pay for the deposits on the tent and the sound and light equipment in lieu of the money coming in later from the ticket sales. Because they had no idea who I was they wouldn't have taken the booking unless I paid a non-refundable amount up front. The tent people wanted €1,500 up front, the sound and light people €2,000. All of this I am not going to see again even though they haven't done anything for it, they've just taken it as a deposit against the full cost which is now not going to happen.

Fucking bollocks isn't it? All this hard work this summer, and to lose it all over one idiot, and it's not like it was my fault. I try to distract myself from thinking about it, when I think about it; I can't stop thinking about it and it makes me angrier and angrier. Ma says I've got to let it go, what has happened has happened and I need to move on or it will eat me up. That's easy for her to say; it's not her who has been humiliated, and anyway she didn't want me to do it in the first place, she said so at the start before changing her tune when it looked like it was going to come off.

I keep playing over in my head the conversation with Toots's tour manager. He went berserk, absolutely berserk, fuck you this and fuck you that: he was an American guy, and started shouting about how he was going to sue me, how we can't fuck him over, how they had bent over backwards to accommodate us.

As if I didn't feel shitty enough, and I just let him shout at me down the phone; there wasn't much I could say back apart from I'm sorry and it wasn't my fault.

He 'didn't give a shit whose fault it was'; he was going to sue me for lost earnings and then I could sue whoever it was whose fault this whole shit storm was.

He kept saying, 'I'm going to shut down your radio station, I'm going to make sure any act I deal with never has anything to do with your organization, your radio station is finished.' He didn't know how right he was.

On the contract I had to sign to book them I put my name as Managing Director, Radio Clifden FM, but if there is no Radio Clifden does that mean the contract isn't worth anything and he can't sue me?

I had put our address as Clifden FM, Treley Road, Clifden.

Now we are 27 Treley Road, so actually he doesn't know where we live, and if he doesn't know where we live he can't actually send us anything to sue us, I think, or I hope. Christ I hope he doesn't sue my parents.

He was shouting, '$200,000, that's how much I'm gonna sue your asses for.'

And $200,000 is enough to make me worry about anything.

45

SATURDAY 2ND SEPTEMBER

Today was supposed to be the day of the festival. Apparently about twenty people turned up at the school; they were probably out-of-towners who hadn't found out it was off.

Padar, the caretaker of the school, who I had organised a lot of the logistics of the event with, called me to let me know. I had thought about going up to the gate and being there to let people know it had been cancelled, but he said he would keep an eye out for anyone and we needn't both be there.

I had gone up earlier in the morning to put a couple of posters up at the school gates with details about how to get a refund.

Apparently it's going to cost €20,000 to repair the damage Davey did. Insurance will cover it, hopefully, but Padar says they haven't said yes yet.

Michelle wanted to meet up again; I didn't want to this time. I knew it would be more of the same.

She had sent me a text saying could she talk to me in her lunch break, so I waited for her at 2.00 p.m. in the car park behind the Super-Value. Embarrassingly it's near one of the white-painted 'PMLV' graffiti bits.

She said she'd agreed to get engaged to Liam, but not to get married; that they wouldn't get a ring until they were getting married. It didn't make sense to me either: you're engaged to be married or you're not. You can't be just engaged, unless you are engaged to be engaged which means you are engaged to be married.

Anyway it sounded like she'd tried to say no to it but he had sort of persuaded her into this compromise.

She basically said the same thing she'd said the last time we met up, about not knowing if she wanted to be with him for the rest of her life, though this time it seemed she was looking for encouragement to break it off with him, for someone to tell her to do it.

I don't know if it was because I was tired of hearing the same stuff all over again or because I leave town on Wednesday so I can pretty much do what I like, but I finally said it. I said, 'Look Michelle, you're a gorgeous girl and I mean gorgeous, you could have any bloke in this town; Christ you could pretty much have any bloke in this country. You only live once: do you want to spend it all with Liam?'

She smiled. 'Thanks Lex, a girl needs to hear that once in a while to feel special.'

I thought fuck it, it's now. If I'm ever going to do it it's going to be now.

I felt bad for betraying Liam but I finally said what I thought, in for the whole lot.

'Look if I were you I'd dump him; you're too good for him, you should just dump him. Any guy would want you, they'd be mad not to, but it's up to you. That's just my thought.

'You are so, so special; he's a nice guy but look at you, you're lovely, Michelle. I'd give my left bollock to go out with a girl like you: actually, with you. I know the feeling's not really the same and I'm cool with that, but I don't want to come back to this town next summer and the summer after and still see you with him, it would be such a waste.'

'Ahh Mister Lex, you say the nicest things,' she says, deflecting.

The blood goes to my face again. I'd basically said all I could short of throwing myself on the floor and proclaiming my undying love for her.

'I'm going now, so here goes. Before I go I am going to kiss you once, just once, just so I know what it's like, and I'm so nice a person that I've told you beforehand so you can leave before I try it so technically I won't have been blown out. OK so I've given you fair warning, right?'

And she didn't leave, and I said, 'Are you sure?' and I leant in and I kissed her on the lips full. I didn't go for tongues or anything but she did open her mouth and it was like three seconds maybe even four or five, and I reached up and I held her boob with my hand. I know, I know, it was magic, and the blood flooded down to my thing, and I said, 'Look I'm really sorry, I just always wanted to do that and I go Wednesday and I just wanted to have done it.'

She smiled again.

'I know you did Lex,' she said and gave me one more kiss on the lips then left, saying, 'You will write to me when you get to London, OK? A proper letter, not email, a letter, per month, from London just to let me know how rude they are.'

Walking home I was buzzing. I went through the conversation again and again; oh man, oooohhh man, she is gorgeous.

The rest of the afternoon I spend sorting my stuff out for London: four days to go.

46

Early Saturday evening, I'm just leaving the house to go into town to get ice cream for Ma for our tea when I see Liam in the distance at the corner just walking onto our street.

It was the way he shouted 'DONAL' that worried me. He calls me Lex, almost everyone calls me Lex, and when I saw him come onto our road that's when he shouted 'DONAL'. At first I didn't know if it was an angry 'DONAL' or a because-I'm-far-away 'DONAL', to get my attention. But I could see him, so he needn't've shouted so loud, and then he started to quicken his pace a bit and he shouts 'DOOOOONAL' again and I think shit, maybe she's actually gone and dumped him this time, he looks bloody angry about it and by the looks of him, he's angry with me. So I started to move up the drive and instinctively, I don't know if it was the guilt, but I started to go the other way from him.

If she's spoken to him who knows what she's said; why would he think it's my fault? Oh shit though, what has she said? Or maybe it's his sister who saw us together in the café, or that kiss: maybe someone saw that kiss and has told him or she admitted it. And so I start to quicken my pace a little and he shouts 'DONAL YOU'RE FUCKING DEAD' and breaks into a run, and I know it's definitely my fault and I start to run too.

I get to the end of the street, burn left and fly across the road, holding my arm out to warn a car to stop. Then right into town past Matherson's; oh fuck I'm dead, I'm dead, I'm really dead. I can hear him shouting behind me and I'm going, I'm going, and I look to see if I'm pulling away from him and I'm not; he's getting nearer, and I pull out from behind one of the cars and I'm going down the middle of the road and I look to see him and he's still coming and his face is red with snot and rage, and when he catches me he's going to kill me. I hope this is some misunderstanding, but it isn't, is it; this is the time I get it, this is the time I get a real and utter beating and I deserve it. I knew I was taking a chance the way I spoke with her, and I knew if it got back to him he would come for me, and I knew it and it happened. I fly into the square looking for places I can get to, or where I could ditch, curl up and let it happen.

I think of shouting wait, and stop, and trying to get him to calm down, but it's not going to happen: we are moving too fast and I realise how physically inferior I am to him and how I'm going to get hurt, badly. I'm like a gazelle who knows the end is coming but keeps running because that's all that's left to do.

Go for the Harp? Too late, we're already past it. I head down the hill for the Super-Value, left for the car park to see if I can get to the path out the back. As I turn left he stretches out a leg and it knocks my left leg onto my right and then I'm flying through the air . . . and then landing, head down, arms outstretched, skidding face first along the tarmac and gravel, and I'm in shock as I hit the ground and let out an 'Arrrggghhh' as I slide into the wall.

I try to get into a ball but he grabs me by my T-shirt and I'm covering my head with my arms. I can feel the bits of gravel on me, rubbing against my face, and he's punching me. He's trying to punch my head but my arm is covering it, then he hits me in the ribs so hard, I mean *so* hard; it hurts like hell and I drop my arm and he pulls his arm back to hit me in the head, but I turn myself down now so he can only hit the back of my head. He's shouting 'WHY'D YOU DO IT? WHY'D YOU DO IT? WHY?' and he's hitting me every time he says why, and he hits my arm, then my body, then my head, then the same arm: WHY? (body) WHY? (head) WHY? A FRIEND? WHY? Then he takes a step back to catch his breath and he's breathing heavily and I think it might be over, but then he takes a step forward, lets out a growl and lines up to kick me, when: CLANK, and he's felled. And he goes straight down, like sparko. It's Davey. Davey has hit him with a metal bin lid and he's knocked him straight out, and he hits him again with it to make sure.

Then Davey is stood over me, and he's breathing hard and I'm trying to breathe but there's blood in my mouth and blood down my arms and I think my ears are bleeding and Davey looks at me; he nods at me, then he runs off.

Eventually I get up, leaving Dansey on the ground. No one has come to see what was happening, so I start to walk home slowly, so slowly; it all aches and a lot of it bleeds. I keep my head down and avoid eye contact with anyone on the way back. I don't know if people saw me fly through town when he was chasing me.

Walking back along the pavement I see Ma scurrying towards me and Fiona is with her and Ma's crying, and when she sees me she cries some more and I don't know if it's because I look worse than she expected or because she's glad I'm alive, but she checks me over and leads me back home.

I tell her someone saved me but I didn't see who it was.

On the way back home she calls Dr Kilpatrick to ask if he can come over and check me out.

Back in the house Ma cleans me up with antiseptic wipes that sting like fuck. She's got me sat on a chair in the kitchen and she sends Fiona and Sean to their rooms. Da doesn't really say anything, just hovers, then calls Peter O'Reilly to tell him what happened.

You know on TV where people refuse to tell the police what happened: well he's my Da's best friend and I've known him all my life so I just told him all of what happened, leaving out that it was Davey who came to my rescue. I said it was some guy.

I even tell him about the Michelle stuff that's a prelude

to it. I sort of admit that maybe I deserved it and I'm not really that hurt, so we'll leave it if that's OK.

He seems fine with that but tells us to call him if anyone turns up again.

I go to my room. I sit with the light off, wondering if Dansey and his crew are going to come back for me, listening to the cars and lights go past my house and wondering if they are outside and want revenge.

This is to be my last night in Clifden and it is spent sat on the floor of my room, back against the radiator under the window, listening for signs of activity outside. The grazes on my arms and face are burning and I'm scared. I'm scared for me, scared for my family, scared for Davey, scared of my hometown. A summer when I was hoping to leave the place as a hero for putting on the best show this place has ever seen, and I'm leaving in fear and embarrassment. What's going to happen to my family when I go; will we have to move? Will Dansey and his mates get at them? Is our name going to be dirt? Have I got them in trouble? I've really fucked things up this time for everyone.

Don't dream, that's what I've learned: don't dream because it's not worth it, or dream in a place no one knows you; that way your failures will be anonymous. No one is going to know me in London: it'll be perfect. I can fail to my heart's content. That's the thing I should have written down.

They say it's better to try and fail than never try at all. I suppose it really depends on the fail though, doesn't it, just how bad is the fail?

Like those blokes who went over Niagara Falls in a barrel and died. I think if you asked them if it was better to try and fail than not try at all, I think if they weren't dead they'd tell you it's better not to try at all.

I wish I'd never bloody tried, I wish I'd never bloody tried with the festival, I wish I'd never bloody tried with Michelle, and I just fucking wish I was out of this town for good.

No one saw Davey do it; Liam never saw it coming. Unless there's CCTV in the car park it might mean he's got away with it, but then it also might mean that Liam thinks it's me that's done it.

I think they must think that's what happened.

I got two texts from Michelle that night. The first said, 'What have you done?'

The second said, 'Are you OK?'

I didn't reply to either. I'm leaving; I'm done with it all. Coward's approach and all that, but fuck it, I can't stick around, it's only going to make things worse. At least with me gone it takes the biggest fool out of the situation. Hopefully things will get back to normal.

I don't know what I was thinking with her anyway; I was an eejit. I knew the consequences of thinking I could mess around with a girl like that, who had a guy like him, and I was stupid enough to go through with it. In all I probably deserved whatever Liam was going to do to me.

You know what I can't stop thinking: I can't stop thinking about this Michelle thing. I knew if I got involved, if anything happened with her, that Liam would bloody kill me. I knew it, my mates warned me, even my ma warned me; and I'm supposed to be a bit of a bright spark, and I knew it would happen, and I bloody went and did it all the same. And yet somehow when it actually did happen, I was surprised.

Like it was a stupid, stupid idea. I knew it was a stupid idea and I couldn't help myself, I had to do it. Like when I touched that electric bar on the heater when I was nine: I knew it would hurt, yet once I started thinking about it I couldn't not do it, and I did it and it hurt, and like, that's how much of an idiot I am.

There's going to be no radio station any more.

I'll shut that all down tomorrow. I'll cancel the mobile for the station too, and throw the SIM card away.

I go and lie on my bed and shut my eyes. Other than worrying about me, I can't stop worrying about Davey: he's got to get out of this town too now. I don't think anyone saw him, but y'know what this town is like: if it gets out he's a dead man, he'll have to leave. He's already a criminal and now he's going to be wanted by Dansey's lot.

I suppose that's us quits, isn't it. He ruined my summer, I've ruined the chance for him to be able to stay in Clifden. Poor lad: losing your mum, your best pal and your town in a summer is a bad run.

47

Lying on my bed, every time I hear a car go past I feel a little sick. I hear some voices outside but it's just a couple walking. At each sound I get up and slide the curtains back a bit to see who it is.

I can hear Ma on the phone downstairs; I don't know who she's talking to at a time like this. It occurs to me that she could be calling her family in Galway for reinforcements. The last thing we need is a fucking gang war over a bloody girl.

Another car goes past outside. I don't know if it's just paranoia but there seems to be a fair few cars going past tonight, like one every five minutes. I mean we're a residential street that leads onto a dead end, so there's not really any through traffic. Most of the cars going past I kind of recognise. None have gone past twice; they're the ones I'm looking for, or those boy-racer cars that Dansey's crew have. If one of them comes past I'm bollixed.

At the end of the road by the corner under the tree I

notice a girl standing there. She's stood in the shadows so isn't easy to see. She could be waiting for someone, but then again she could be a lookout; it could be Dansey's sister. The girl by the tree has long dark hair but after a bit pulls her hood up. Why would you have your hood up if you weren't up to something shifty?

I give it five minutes, which in the end turns out to be less than two, then call Da from downstairs.

'You OK boy?' he says when he gets into my room. He turns the light on, which I immediately turn off, so they can't see me from outside.

I tell Da about the girl under the tree by the end of the road and how dodge it seems. Ma comes up the stairs and wants to know what's going on. We tell her about the girl and that we think it's Liam's sister.

'Want me to get Peter to check it out?' she says.

'No, leave it Ma, we could just send Da out for a walk to see if he recognises them,' I say.

'That's very brave of you Lex,' says Da.

I know what he means but I don't want Peter to be involved if he doesn't have to be. It might be nothing, but then the more I look out the window the more suspicious it seems.

Ma then decides to take control of the situation, telling Da to walk out there, walk past the girl, then walk round the corner and come back. If you recognise her or anything you come straight back.

'Ma, he doesn't know what Liam's sister looks like.'

'OK: you walk past, have a look, come back and describe

her and if we think it's her we'll call Peter and get him to go out and talk to her.'

Da goes downstairs to stick his coat and shoes on. Me and Ma look from the window. Da goes out the drive and right and stays on this side of the road before crossing at the end, giving him a decent look at her. As he's walking past she seems to say something to him and he stops, and he's talking to her, and he stays talking to her. Then he turns to come back and she follows a bit behind.

I go down the stairs and Da comes in and says, 'There's someone to see you.' Then it clicks: that might have been Michelle out there, but it couldn't have been; the hair seemed straight and I'd have recognised the figure.

The back door opens into the kitchen and what is stood there is either a very ugly girl or a very ugly long-haired guy.

I look again at the slightly kinked nose and ask, 'Davey?'

And it's him, in some kind of dodgy wig disguise.

'Davey? Is that you?'

'All right kiddo?' he says and smiles an embarrassed smile. 'You OK?' he asks.

And it clicks where he's got the wig from. I feel slight nausea as I realise it's probably the wig his mum was wearing when she was having her treatment.

That's fucking sick.

'Yeah, yeah, cool,' I say. 'You?'

'Yeah, good, yeah.'

Ma and Da leave the kitchen and the two of us are just stood there and stuck with a silence. Eight years of being best mates and suddenly we've got nothing to say to each other.

Like, literally nothin'.

'Just wanted to see if you were all right, man,' he says.

'Yeah, I'm good, man, I'm good. Thanks for earlier, man.'

'No bother,' he says, 'just wanted to make sure you were OK, like.'

'I'm good, I'm good,' I say, 'but I'm going to have to leave tomorrow. We're, y'know, bringing things forward a bit. Ma thinks it's for the best.'

'Cool, man, cool.'

'We fucked this one up didn't we?' I say and smile.

'Yeah totally,' he says and lets out a laugh.

'I don't know what you're laughing about, bud, you're the one who's going to have to face the music. I'll be gone.'

'Ah it'll be cool, no worries.'

I don't know how he can be so confident: he's just nearly killed someone with a bin lid and they are going to want revenge.

'I gotta go. I just wanted to check you were OK,' he says.

'Cool, yeah, cool.'

'OK, well see ya,' he says.

'Yeah, see ya, bud.'

And he gives me this soppy look, so then I say, 'Come here, man,' and I step out the back door and open up my arms to him.

He sticks his head down and we hug. Proper hug. Him being a bit of short-arse his head goes under my chin, and I give him a full-on squeeze and he squeezes back and then, being the jessie I am, I start to cry. I'm going to miss him so much; we've done everything together since we became best buds in middle school. We've been in trouble; we've got out of trouble; we've passed hours – thousands and thousands of hours – together, just killing time and doing nothing and everything and anything.

I hope he's going to be OK.

I sob into his ear.

'You take care of yourself, yeah?'

He pulls back from the hug and smiles at me. 'Yeah, right.'

Then he turns and goes.

And it clicks: the times he's protected me, his being there when Liam attacked me, him outside the pub earlier in the summer. He's always been there for me, always been there protecting me. There's me thinking that I'm the one easing his transition into society and looking out for him and he was there all along. And even tonight he's out there, making sure I'm all right. I blub a bit more.

He's fearless, he's selfless, he's an idiot but he's my idiot. Jesus, Davey, you're a good lad, and I know I'm going to struggle in London without my own short-fuse guardian angel to look after me.

I worry right then that our friendship is going to change; things will be different between us once I go away, once I go to this new life. We may never be friends like this again; I may never meet another friend like him again. But we did rule.

*

I stayed up until after 2.30 a.m. I was waiting to see if anything would happen after the pubs kicked out, if anyone would come by, but nothing happened.

48

SUNDAY 3RD SEPTEMBER

Ma shouts it's time to leave. Breakfast has been had in silence, with even Fiona keeping quiet.

I have my printed slate-grey Richard Pryor T-shirt on. Never worn before, got it from Zhivago Records. I always knew it was what I was going to wear when I went to London. Stan Smiths are on too.

I go up to get my bag. From downstairs Fiona has started; she's begging Ma to let her come to the airport with us. Ma gives in easily this time. She picks her battles.

I take a look at the room and the computer that has been my life for the last two years. In front of it sits the mixing desk. It was never supposed to end like this. It was supposed to end in celebration. It was supposed to end with me closing down the radio station and thanking everyone for helping make it all happen. I would play the Maytals' 'Country Roads' as my last-ever song and sail off into the sunset, no doubt with the whole town waving me off at the carnival they threw in honour of my departure, as I went to discover new lands.

But it doesn't end like that. For a second I think of booting up the PC just once more and doing a final broadcast, but it passes and I head back downstairs dragging the bag after me.

We load up the car and I say a mental goodbye to the house. I get to sit up front with Da, a rare honour. Ma, Fiona and Sean are slotted in the back.

FIONA

Lex is in so much trouble. He has to go away early because he will get beaten up if he doesn't. I feel really bad for him. I just hope that he is safe. They won't go to London to get him. I knew he was making a mistake with that girl. I could have told him it wouldn't have worked out, but Lex would not have listened to me so he had to learn the bad way.

Mum said we couldn't go to the airport with them but we have to, as that's where I am going to give him the biggest hug ever and it wouldn't be as special here.

I am going to miss him.

SEAN

I'm glad Lex is going.

It means no more rubbish dead arms, and no more me

having to do whatever Mum and Dad want to keep him happy.

Davey has said he'll look after me when Lex goes, which is brilliant cos having Davey about will mean I'm safe and no one can get me again and Lex never did that. I am going to get Lex's room too and his computers.

When he comes back home I hope he's not so grumpy all the time.

I can't believe I can't stay at home and we all have to go to the airport.

LEX

I haven't mentioned it, but Da drives like he's on a low dose of morphine. He drives slow and steady, like a catatonic koala bear. He backs the car out and I'm finally leaving.

We turn left out of our road and are just about to go left again onto the Galway Road when Ma shouts out, 'Keep driving!' I'd been trying to sort the CD player and didn't know why she shouted, so looked up and saw Michelle was on the pavement walking up towards our house. Ma shouts, 'Keep driving!' again, and Da does what he's told and pulls out quickly onto the main road.

I see her and she sees me see her, but it's quick, and her look is like 'Wait,' or at least I think it is, and that's why Ma wants us not to stop.

Da carries on driving. There's going to be no stopping or going back and I don't even argue it.

Two minutes later my phone buzzes with a text. I open it up and it's from Michelle. It says:

Michelle
03/09/2006, 09:48:03
I need to talk to you.

I look at the text again.

And again.

And again.

And then I delete it.

Nothing good will come from talking to her.

It's time to move on, it's time for London, it's time for a new beginning; this stuff, this trouble and her have to be behind me. I need to be gone.

* * *

The actual goodbye at the airport was worse than I'd thought. You have to remember I've been planning this escape for two years and have built this moment up. This isn't a goodbye, this is a hello: this is hello London, this is hello world and this is hello to the rest of my life. I've done my time in the town and now it's time to move on. I haven't left as I would have liked, but the important thing is I'm leaving: but when the moment arrived I suddenly didn't feel ready.

The five of us queued up for the check-in desk, lined up behind one old fella in lemon slacks. I did the check-in part on my own. Ma and Da were stood close behind me explaining it was just one person travelling and they were just here to see me off. I could hear Fiona asking Sean if he knew how to spell 'moron' then spelling it out for him. Usually Ma tells her off when she teases him but she was fixated on me, and helping me load up my bag onto the travelator–weighing thing.

Once I was done we all went to the security gate. The plane wasn't leaving for another eighty minutes and Ma asked if I wanted them to wait with me. I told them best not, that I'd just go on through and get myself something to read.

She touched the grazing on my face; it still stung from the bastard gravel behind the Super-Value, and she apologised as I winced.

'Family hug!' she called, and with that the four of them all crowded round me to give me an almighty squeeze. I nearly cried at that point. I didn't though. Ma did, I heard her sniff into my chest.

And that was it. A big exaggerated wave as I went through to security. They kept waving back as I showed my passport and were still doing it until the last point they could see me, and then I was through and into the queue for the hand-luggage scanners.

When I was in the queue I could actually still see them on a monitor which showed the camera view of the concourse. They were still stood there for a while, waiting as if I might come back for one final wave. And then the strangest thing happened. I saw Fiona give Sean a hug. I've never seen Fiona give Sean a hug in my life. She's given Sean a hug, and then given Ma a hug, then given Da a hug. Da has given Ma a hug and gave Sean a hug too. And I was thinking, so is that it? I've gone two bloody seconds and they've already changed as a family.

Remember I said I was a little bit 'famous' in the town because of the radio station? I did, I said it back on page 113. I'm not: I'm not famous at all; I'm famous in my own head. When I'm gone, I'll be gone. I kind of thought when I left there would be this big hole in Clifden where I had been, but there won't; there won't even be a hole in my family. People move and adapt to fill the gap when someone leaves.

Seconds after I had said goodbye to them, the family was already readjusting to fill the hole where I had been. Fiona will just get bigger and more relentless within the unit. Sean will grow too; I wouldn't be surprised if he started hanging out with Davey more. He's not stopped going on about him for the last few days: how Davey's great and Davey's going to look after him. Davey will play football with him when he wants and besides they've got the same mental age, so they'll get on.

Michelle and Liam will sort themselves out. Whatever yesterday was about, I bet they'll be back together before the week's out. They are meant for each other: neither of them wants to leave that town and good luck to them. I'm just sorry I messed them all around; I was selfish and didn't appreciate the trouble I was causing.

Clifden will still go on. There is going to be no hole

where I once was that won't be filled; it'll be as if the radio station never existed. Maybe that was why I wanted to put on the festival; maybe it was one big vanity show for me, to leave an impression. Maybe Fiona was right; maybe I am a narcissist. She is a bright girl after all.

I sat there reading the *Sunday Indo* at the gate, realizing the little impact I'd had on Clifden, when an announcement comes on that our flight will be delayed for twenty-five minutes as there has been an emergency landing at the airport and it will take a short time to clear the runway.

A few minutes later I hear an airport engineer shouting into his mobile. I get a bit of it: he says, '. . . Yeah, yeah . . . no, apparently it's a private jet . . . yeah . . . yeah . . . took off from Dublin . . . mechanical problems or something . . . emergency landing . . . repair it . . . sending for someone . . . no, no . . . yeah . . . apparently it's that fucking Bono . . .'

Author's Note

The Clifden in the story is a fictionalised version of the town in Connemara, Ireland. It is a lovely town should you ever wish to visit it, and Connemara is the most beautiful place.

In memory of LSM – a good man

Acknowledgements

Caroline Dawnay and Olivia Hunt at United. Jedi Jon Riley, Charlotte Clerk, Jenny Ellis and all at Quercus. JT & Stella, Alex Rayner, Jane Whittaker, Marie Ronn, Jessica Craig, Jane Willis and Zoe Ross.